The Reckoning

By

Ronald C. Williamson

and

Carolyn Clark

Illustrations by

Eric Keith Williamson

THE RECKONING

Copyright © 2014

ISBN: 978-0-692-29889-3

Registered with the Library of Congress

Published by:

Ronald\Williamson

136 Homewood Drive

Millbrook, AL 36054-2340

USA

DEDICATION

This novel is dedicated to the illustrator of this book, Eric Keith Williamson, beloved brother of Ronald Williamson. Keith was voted by students as one of the best teachers in the school at the University of Mississippi where he taught.

Eric Keith Williamson

1956 - 2014

Foreword

My beloved husband, Ronald Craig Williamson, is a throwback in time, a true southern gentleman. He is traditional, polite, considerate, and God fearing. If I had to place Ron in a decade where his values were the most befitting, I would say the early 1840s.

My mother, Carolyn Faye Clark, is the epitome of individualism. To say she marches to the beat of her own drummer does not even scratch the surface. She holds strongly to her beliefs, traditional or not. The 1960s would be the era in which I feel my mother would feel most able to express herself and she was fortunate enough to live during that decade.

It would seem that my husband and mother being caught in two very different Eras might be at odds. Yet they have collaborated to tell a story that emphasizes what they both place at the center of their lives, their love of Jesus Christ, our Lord and Savior.

Susannah L. Williamson

THE RECKONING

Prologue

But as it is written, "What no eye has seen, nor ear heard nor the human heart conceived, what God has prepared for them who love Him... these things God has revealed to us through the Spirit; for the Spirit searches everything, even the depth of God". I Corinthians 2:9-10

I was created eons ago before roads and houses, businesses and farms, animals or even mankind ever came to Greenwood, Mississippi. Actually, there was no Greenwood, Mississippi. There was only blistering heat, freezing cold and the stirrings of my life in the mind of God. I am twenty-seven. The year is 1986.

Chapter 1

I am the child of Virginia and Herston Carrington, that is to say the only living child. There were two before me who never knew the world outside the dark warmth of our mother's body and another, born two years after me, who felt the secure embrace of our parent's arms for only two short days before she too was gone. I am not an only child; I just grew up that way. Therefore, all the love, nurturing, guidance and direction that could have been spread amongst four children have been given to me. I have accepted it mostly with gratitude, but during my younger years, I at times felt the weight of it somewhat smothering. But now that I'm past those growing up years, I recognize just how fortunate I am to have been born into this family. The value of my upbringing will become far more evident as my tale unfolds.

Greenwood is situated in the Mississippi delta region in a flood zone area where the Tallahatchie River from the north meets the Yalobusha River from the east to form the Yazoo River running south.

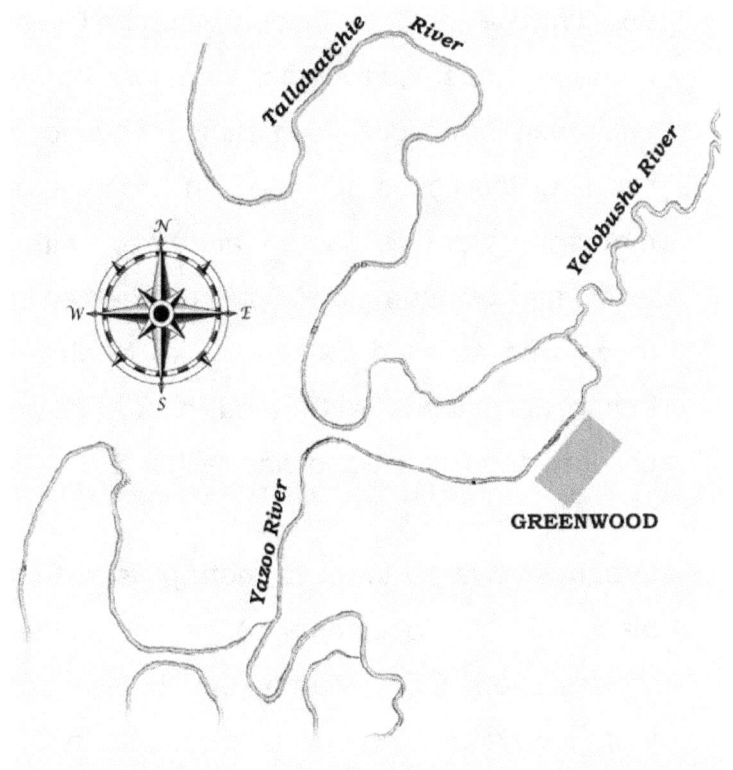

This makes for rich, fertile farmland but also an abundance of marshy swampland. The lower areas flood during excessive rainfall. Like other farmers around us my father wisely had our house built atop the highest ground on our acreage. Twice in my lifetime the flooding has been so bad that all I could see below our house for miles around was a roadway on built-up high ground snaking through the acres of floodwater with occasional rooftops of distant farmhouses breaking the horizon. Those were bad years for farmers. Crops and livestock were lost, homes and equipment damaged, sometimes beyond repair. But after the floods subsided, the soil was richer, the crops were re-planted and grew with more vigor, and our community pulled together to help those who suffered damage. Like Noah and his family after the Great Flood, God blessed his children and Greenwood was restored.

Greenwood is no teeming metropolis. In fact, no place in Mississippi teems, at least not in the ways of New York City, Atlanta, or Chicago. And for that, we who love our quiet southern life are thankful. Mississippians have ever-expanding Jackson where commerce and trade move energetically forward. Oxford and Starkville are home to universities nationally noted as centers of higher education and college football, the glue that binds the South together as tightly as do magnolia trees and sweet iced tea. Along the Gulf Coast of the state are towns and villages devoted to fishing and an industry growing around it. And that's enough for me. My Mississippi is a world of forests, meadows, swamplands, and dark waterways. Its home and I love it.

I was raised at Carrington Farms, an eight hundred acre tract with prime river bottomland. The farm did not start out so large two generations ago when Herston Carrington Senior brought his young bride Amelia Mae Sutherland here from her ancestral home in Alabama. They met when she came to visit her Aunt Lettie and Uncle Boyce Marshall in the spring of 1931. Amelia was the sheltered daughter of a Baptist preacher and had never been so far from home. But at age 19, she was allowed to make the trip with members of her father's little congregation who were visiting relatives nearby. It was at a barn-raising that Amelia first met Herston. From the moment they met, he knew he had found his life-mate. Her feelings for him were not far behind. By the time she was to return home a month later, they were determined to be man and wife. Herston Sr. made the return trip to Alabama with Amelia to meet her parents. The Reverend and Mrs. Sutherland had been forewarned by both Amelia and the Marshalls of the impending visit and suspected the reason behind it. A nervous but stalwart Herston withstood the introductions and subsequent questioning well. The Sutherlands could see the love glowing around these two young people. Herston was honest to a fault admitting that he owned little more than the proverbial forty acres and a mule. He had a milk cow, a few chickens, a small dwelling, big dreams and a strong back. But even more importantly, he had an unmovable and abiding faith in God and never doubted that his dreams would materialize if it was God's will. The Sutherlands could see his faith in everything he said and did. Reverend Sutherland joined his daughter and Herston in marriage, and a week later the couple set out for their home in Mississippi with their eyes on God and a shining future. God did not disappoint them.

After more than fifty years of toil and tilling this soil, my Pappaw Herston had amassed two hundred and fifty acres of fruitful land, a sizable herd of cattle, two daughters and two sons, my father Herston Junior being the eldest child. Within months of the passing away of my Mammaw Amelia at age 71, Pappaw followed her leaving behind a reputation for fairness, honesty and a solid Christian life lived in service to God. Those who knew him through his trade within the community, his service to his neighbors and those in need, or as a member of Greenwood Baptist Church, never had to be told of his strong Christian faith. Pappaw Herston lived it all day, every day. And from the day he could first toddle about, my father walked in Pappaw's footsteps along that pathway set out by the Hand of God. That is how my father learned to be a farmer and tend the land my Pappaw had poured so many years of love and sweat into. And its how my father learned to be a man and the head of his own family.

My father married a woman of faith as is taught in the Bible. Virginia Elizabeth Wetherby grew up in Greenwood just like my father did. They knew each other from childhood through our church. Virginia attended a private school for girls in Hattiesburg during the week and was at home only on week-ends and holidays. She and my father only saw each other on Sundays and maybe church socials on the occasional Saturday. It wasn't until mother had finished her last year at school that they actually became well acquainted. Over the summer following mother's graduation from school, they began dating and by spring were in love. Being two years older than Mother, Father was completing his second year of agricultural studies at Mississippi State when he asked her to be his wife. After they were married they moved into the big, rambling farmhouse where the Carrington's had shared multi-generational life since Pappaw and Mammaw first established their home. Over the years rooms had been added to their little house as children came along. And when those children took spouses, the expansions continued. It was my father who finally chose a plot of land near the original home-place to build a new house for his family. He flourished as a husband, then a father, and the farm prospered.

The house my dad had built is a big, rambling structure. It has two stories and five bedrooms to accommodate the large family he and my mother had hoped to have. The downstairs has a large entryway with a center stairway leading up to the second floor. To the left of the entryway is the living room with French doors down the side wall opening onto a wide veranda that encircles the entire house. On the back wall of the living room is a sizable fireplace with a black walnut surround and mantle that was salvaged from an old plantation house built in the early 1800's. Beyond the living room is my father's study and the master suite my parents share. To the right of the entry is a formal dining room. Behind that is a butler's pantry fashioned after those in old English manor houses. Ours is used to store china, table linens and such although our household does not include an actual butler. Behind the pantry is the heart of the house…our kitchen. It's really big with plenty of room for cooking, canning and all the many tasks a southern farm family does. It's where we eat breakfast and lunch and even the occasional evening meal. We joke that we have dinner in the dining room but supper in the kitchen. Off the back of the kitchen is my mother's favorite room…the sunroom. It's her refuge from a busy household. She has comfortable chintz covered couches and chairs among her beloved house plants and her most favorite spot of all, her chaise. The upstairs of the house is divided by the stairwell with two bedrooms on either side. My room is the front bedroom on the right. I like that spot because I can see the driveway and anyone who comes or goes to and from the house and it's also very quiet except during dinner.

We were a Christian family and attended Greenwood Southern Baptist Church regularly. We prayed daily and at all meals. Through Bible study at church and at home, I learned Christian doctrine and was expected at all times to abide by the teachings of Jesus. I was taught from a young age that Jesus is the Son of God, that he had been born of the Virgin Mary and that he taught love, charity and service to others. I learned the story of his death on the cross and that he had risen three days later. Father explained that this all took place to redeem us from our sins. As I grew older I came to understand that Jesus Christ would return again someday to gather unto himself all the Christians who believed. I knew that we should all be ready for and look forward to his return.

Father was a very spiritual man who lived the teachings of Jesus. He was ardent in efforts to ensure my understanding and following the tenets of Christianity especially as they applied to the treatment of others. He told me time and again that the greatest commandment is to love the Lord our God with our whole heart. And he taught me the second greatest commandment is to love others as we love ourselves. He was always showing his love for others through the many things he did to help all who needed him while expecting nothing in return. My father was also a great believer in, "turning the other cheek". He frequently quoted I Thessalonians 5:15 which says, "See that none render evil for evil unto any man; but ever follow that which is good, both among yourselves, and to all men". When someone did Father wrong, he did not retaliate because he believed that revenge was reserved only for God. Although I had accepted Jesus as my Savior at an early age and truly believed in living the Christ-like life, I still had trouble with turning the other cheek. I had long discussions with my dad about my desire to exact justice for myself. He would always remind me that God is all-powerful and can exact far more severe judgment than I could, and he'd say, "Leave it in the Lord's hands, Ron. Leave it in his hands."

Mother was a sparkling, out-going woman. She was a beautiful girl when my father married her and has become even more beautiful as she matured. Her dark hair waves and curls gracefully around her oval face. Her hazel eyes sparkle with intelligence, humor and just the slightest hint of mischief. Mother has always been graceful and has an air of calm about her. Her hands are capable yet gentle. She is the epitome of a strong, cultured southern lady. She and my father make a handsome couple. He stands a head taller than mother and is as solid and sturdy as she is ephemeral. His jet black hair is thick and straight. And his eyes are so dark that it is difficult to detect their pupils within the iris. His eyes are not fierce, however, being softened by the laugh lines at their outer corners. His ready smile put those lines there. Father's hands are huge and are rough and calloused from years of farm work. But a touch from his hands can still to this day make me feel safe and protected.

Although mother had no job outside the home, she was always busy with her various clubs and activities. She was active in the local VFW Auxiliary. My father was a VFW member and had served in the U.S. Navy in World War II and in the U.S. Marines in Korea. She was an avid gardener and a member of the Greenwood Roses, the local gardening club. Mother also was the leader of the 4-H Club in Greenwood. But her favorite activity, and the one to which she gave the most time and attention, was the girl's Sunday School Class at our church. She, like my father, studied the Bible diligently and took her responsibilities of service to

God very seriously. She played as strong a part as did Father in opening my mind to God.

As did my parents and their ancestors, and following the tenets of the Christian faith, I believe the Bible is the inspired and infallible word of God; the Trinity of the Godhead being the Father, Son and Holy Ghost; creation of man was by the direct act of God; the fall and sin nature of man; Jesus, the only son of God, was born of the Virgin Mary and was sinless; Jesus willingly gave his life to pay the sin debt of man; Jesus was resurrected on the third day and lives for evermore, and that through his grace all who confess their sin and ask for forgiveness and believe will be re-born with the Holy Spirit dwelling within them; and that Jesus will gather together all Christians to be with him for evermore and all others who do not accept his free gift of salvation will be forever doomed to hell. My family shared our faith with others and tried to make our lives reflect the love of Jesus for all mankind. I endeavor to live that life still today. But I remember a time when I should have tried harder, a lot harder.

Chapter 2

After it was confirmed that my mother was carrying me, her doctor in Greenwood decided to consult with some obstetrics specialists at University Hospital. It was decided that in order to avoid the tragedy of another lost child, Mother should stay off her feet as much as possible until my birth. Although she says it reminded her of the obligatory months of confinement impressed on women in generations preceding her, she agreed. She knew this time that for her it was not about doing things by the social correctness of bygone days but with the safety of her unborn child. That is when Alma Bogan came into her life.

Alma was a tall, angular woman with large hands and feet. Her back was ramrod straight and she walked as though she was always late to where she was going. Her brown eyes were set in a round ebony face surrounded by a halo of close-cropped black curls. On first glance she looked stern and distant, but when she smiled it was like a sunrise had lit her from within. According to Mother, Alma immediately upon being hired to help care for her and the household chores, settled in like she'd always been there. She'd arrive each morning before "Mr. Herston" had to get out to the fields and stayed until supper had been eaten and the kitchen cleaned. She cared for my mother as if she were her own child. Mother often tells little stories about Alma's fussing over her and pampering her. Mother says she couldn't even slip out to take a walk around the yard without Alma's warning, "Now Miss Virginia, you know what your doctor said about being off your feet. If you just have to have a turn around the flower garden, wait a minute while I get the wheelbarrow!" Mother says they'd both laugh and she'd plop back down on a lawn chair or the chaise in the sunroom. Mother said there was just no slipping away from Alma. Personally, I think Alma is like all women with eyes in the back of her head. I know my mother has them. I discovered that early on in my childhood and am quickly learning that my wife Rachel has them too. We've been married only a year, but I already know. Heaven help this child we're expecting in a few months.

Alma is married to Eutus Bogan, a local mechanic/carpenter/whatever you need done kind of man. He is short, rotund, always laughing and stronger than men twice his size. By the time Eutus came into my family's life, he was already well known and admired in the community for his many abilities and for doing what he said he would do when he said he would do it. Alma and Eutus had not been blessed with children during their twelve year marriage, a source of disappointment for them both. But they didn't question the will of God on the matter but chose rather to give their time and energy through the outreach of the AME Zion Church.

Eutus worked with the boys in the church and surrounding community doing anything from coaching ball teams to organizing community clean-up days and providing any help needed by the ill and elderly. He kept the boys busy under his watchful eye and encouraged them to fulfill their Christian duties to their community. And more than one of his boys could profess to the severity of the tongue lashing Eutus could deliver when school grades fell or improper behavior occurred. But the boys loved and respected him because they knew he cared. Over the years Eutus Bogan saved many a lad from following a destructive path.

Alma's contribution to her church was mostly quiet work. She saw to it that the sanctuary of the small white cinder block building was immaculately clean for every service. The floors and pews showed not a speck of dust, the windows sparkled and the altar was always banked with flowers fresh cut from yards, meadows and roadsides during the warm months. In cold weather, glossy holly twigs, cedar branches and magnolia leaves showed their winter glory. So no matter when the doors opened in that little church, the fragrance was a mixture of lemon oil, musty hymnals, Johnson's Paste Wax, and plants of the season, all from the hands of Alma's quiet work. But as the church choir stood to begin a service in song, Alma was no longer quiet. Her rich contralto voice sprang forth leading them in songs of praise and thanksgiving to God who had lead them all to this place of worship.

I don't see Alma as often now as I used to before I moved out of the house. Some days I'd like to step back in time and spend an afternoon playing with clothespin soldiers she made for me with their penciled in faces and uniforms. They stood at attention along the rows of clean towels and bed linens on the backyard clothes-line. Some of them even made it to the ground to do battle in the grass and gravel around the back steps. Once those ground soldiers left Alma's clothespin bag, they could never return to it. "Mind you, Ron! Don't go putting those fighting men back in with my clean pins. I don't want that battlefield dirt on my clean washing," she'd chuckle. I cherish those good times, but its Alma's working hands and that rich, soothing voice that I first think of when she comes to mind. But I also remember what she did for my mother and father during the most frightening time of their lives.

Chapter 3

Growing up in Greenwood, Mississippi was like growing up in Wonderland for a boy like me. I always liked being outside. Being confined to the house was torture. I craved the woods, waterways, and unconstrained freedom. Alma often remarked that even as an infant, my fussy times would go away as soon as she got me into fresh air. She teasingly told my mother that all that stillness inside the house before I was born had an impact forever on me. I'd never feel right unless I was outside. Maybe she was partly right. All I know is that any time I could be outside, I was. Although I was a good student and enjoyed my studies, my teachers noticed that I always wanted a desk closest to the row of windows in the classroom. I was the last one back inside after recess and the first out the door at the end of the school day. After school when homework and chores were finished, I'd head outside. I always enjoyed climbing trees when I was younger and would go up into them as high as possible. I learned from near-falls to pay attention when the thinner limbs near the tops would bend or when the wind was too strong to dare go any higher.

I liked scouting around searching for game in anticipation of the different hunting seasons. I would test my strength and agility against any barriers or challenges I could find. I'd try to get lost in the woods just so I could practice finding my way out again. With permission from my parents, I'd spend the night alone camping without conveniences like matches, blankets or food. I wanted to learn to survive on my wits and knowledge, to be self-sufficient. Especially on my first such trek, I had to learn to control fear and panic, both enemies of self-reliance. And learn I did.

I remember a particular water adventure especially well. I was hiking along the Tallahatchie River. This river was known for its rapid current, undertow and whirlpools. It was a fact known around Greenwood that people had drowned while swimming in the river. They were caught unawares and sucked under its murky surface to rise much later and much further downstream. But

I always wanted to prove myself able to conquer it. As I look back now, I see the foolishness of my actions, but by divine providence alone, am I here to tell the story.

As I walked along the river bank, I noticed a log on the ground. That's when the idea hit me. I pulled off my shoes and tied the laces together in a firm knot. Then I slung them over my shoulder. I rolled the log to the edge of the river and scooted down the bank easing the log into the water. I slipped into the water holding onto the log and started swimming toward the other side. The water was perpetually so muddy you couldn't see more than an inch below the surface. As I swam I remembered the loggerhead turtle I snagged while netting for fish along the riverbank. That thing was huge! Its shell must have been three feet wide because I could sit on it. Then it occurred to me that there was no way I could see what or when something could swim along and take a chunk out of me. That's about the time I started swimming a little harder...hoping to go faster. I'd known the current would carry me downstream as I crossed the water, but my guesstimate was off quite a bit. I made it across in one piece, but I had an extra hour of walking to do to get back to Money Road, cross the bridge over the Tallahatchie and then back home. But you know, I didn't mind that walk one bit. There's nothing like another adventure resting under a teenage boy's belt to make a day brighter.

Because my parents raised me in the safety of a small community, I had freedom to roam. Before I was old enough to drive, I would bicycle all over Greenwood and its surrounding farms on my own paths and shortcuts. When I took to the roadways, I took curves sharper and quicker than cars could by leaning my bike low into the turns. I seemingly knew no fear when it came to my bike riding. Once I decided to build a ramp for doing long jumps. There was a large pile of sand at the end of our driveway at home. Behind it was a row of privet hedges. I used bricks to build a ramp up the sand pile. I'd start a good ways back and get up speed before I hit the brick ramp then, at the top of the ramp, pull up on the handlebars to raise the front of my bike. I'd then go sailing over the privet and land on the back lawn. One day I was evidently not in my best form because I failed to pull up on the bike as I crested the ramp. After clearing the hedge, the bikes front tire headed toward the ground first and I tumbled head over heels across the grass. Fortunately for me, it was a cold day so I was bundled up in coat, hat and gloves. I came out of that incident a little stunned and bleeding from a cut over my right eye. To this day, I'm still not sure what caused the cut.

Despite all my daring on the roads and ramps, the worst bike accident I ever had was on a sidewalk. I ran over a stick which then flipped up and got stuck in the spokes of my front tire. The tire rotated until the stick lodged into the fork of the bike frame. The front wheel instantly stopped turning, the back of the bike reared up off the ground, and I went flying over the handlebars into a thorny rose bush. I came out with some scratches and a bruised ego because what made that my worst accident ever was a carload of girls from school happened to be riding by just in time to witness the entire performance.

I've always loved going fishing. While growing up I often tagged along with anyone around who had a fishing rod in his or her hand. Ponds, streams, rivers or canals all were fine with me so long as I could fish them. Alma liked to fish as much as I did and many happy hours were spent with her catching bream and catfish for that night's supper. And that lady knew what to do with fresh fish and a big iron skillet. Those meals were my favorites...fish, grits, coleslaw, and hushpuppies that would melt the minute I bit into those crusty round balls of deliciousness. As I grew older I would go fishing on my own. But somehow, those days with Alma sitting on the warm ground by the water listening to her hum softly the old spirituals from her youth, are some of my dearest fishing memories. It's funny how those quiet times often outshine the days when you caught that eight pound bass out of Pappaw's pond.

Everything in nature fascinated me. Trees, plants, insects, reptiles; they all needed to be watched, studied, cross-referenced and understood. The dive-bombing B-52 mosquitoes so prevalent in the Mississippi Delta, hurt when they stung but I needed to know more about them. The burning between my shoulder-blades from the packsaddle when I'd be working beside Father in the corn fields didn't douse my interest. The warning buzz of a rattlesnake in blackberry patches along the fence row could stop me cold in my tracks, but as it finally slithered away I would follow and watch its graceful motion. And then there were the stars.

It was Father who first piqued my fascination with stars. One summer night I was stretched out on the fresh cut grass in our backyard staring up into the night sky. Father came out and joined me. We laid there in silence for a few minutes; our time together was always special to us both. When he finally spoke he said, "Ron, do you know which one is the North Star?" "Hmm, no sir, I don't think I do." "Well son, can you see the Big Dipper?" "Yes sir, I see it." I said while I shook my head in the affirmative. "If you follow the two stars forming the cup of the Big Dipper, they'll point you to the North Star." I looked for a minute and then saw what he meant. "I see it! Right there!" I said pointing. "Do you know what's so important about the North Star, Ron?" he asked. I was quiet because I didn't have an answer. Father continued, "If you find the North Star then you know where north is. That means you will never really be lost because if you know which way is north, you can determine which direction leads home." Little did I know how important that first astrology lesson learned on a warm summer night would prove to be until some years later.

Chapter 4

Father was a hunter as were many of his friends and other family members. But he did not trophy hunt. He respected all of God's creatures, and killed only what we could eat. That lesson was drilled into me over and over again. When I got my first BB gun for Christmas at age 9, I knew it was for targets...and birds, squirrels, and cats were not targets.

A few years later I got my first "man's gun", a Marlin .22 semiautomatic rifle, and the same rules still applied. Other than animals for food I could only kill if my quarry posed a threat to my life or that of another human, pet or farm animal. The only exception to that rule was the rats that feasted on the animal feed kept in the barn and corncrib. However, the barn cats and a few resident snakes did a pretty good job of keeping the rat population under control around the barn and other outbuildings.

As all hunters do, Father and his brother, my Uncle David, liked to sit around and talk about hunting trips and their various kills. Sometimes it seemed like a contest of who shot the biggest or most of whatever they were after. Before he died, Pappaw Herston was usually the one with a story to top all others. After he was gone, it became a ritual between his two sons but always with good humor and lots of joking and laughter. I loved being on the edges of those conversations when I was a boy. I listened with anticipation of that glorious day in my future when I could do more than just hear the tales. It was a proud day when I finally could chime in to announce my day's kill of three rabbits. My Uncle David cracked, "Well Boy, if your Mamma and Alma can rustle up enough biscuits and gravy and mashed potatoes to go with three rabbits, you have brought home supper!" I felt ten feet tall and knew I didn't have to lurk around the edges ever again...I had become part of the almighty hunter's inner circle.

Soon squirrels and rabbits were not enough for me. I wanted to become a deer hunter, a big man, the real deal. I took to the woods every spare minute I had. I searched for deer paths through the trees and soon discovered that the best way to find a path was to begin at a watering spot and work backward from there. Even though it was early springtime and deer season was months away, I wanted to be ready for the season of my fourteenth year. I quickly learned how the deer paths crisscrossed our land from pools of spring water to barely visible bedding spots in the woods to the outer edges of Mother's flower beds and to the corn fields. I quickly saw the reason for the extra high fence around the kitchen garden that Mother and Alma worked so hard to cultivate. From it came almost all the vegetables our family ate. Father contributed sweet corn, peas, watermelons and pumpkins from his fields, but the rest came from the women. And oh did those deer evermore love those flowers and vegetables.

We didn't have many fruit trees, but those neighbors who did were in constant battle with the deer for the fruit. One neighbor, Caleb Bruin, had a rather sizeable orchard. After years of struggling to outsmart the foraging deer, he announced he'd finally made peace with them over his apples and pears. "They can have all 'a them pears and apples they want as fahr up as they kin reach. I jest wish the durned peaches weren't so low to tha ground", he grumbled.

I enjoyed those times when it was harvest season for our pecans around late fall. I would climb in the trees, jump up and down on branches and shake the limbs around me so the pecans would fall to the ground. It made for some interesting times when it would start lightly snowing and the cold north wind would be howling through the trees. I never fell out of the trees though, which I can say now I am amazed I didn't. We would gather bags full of pecans and then came the slow process of shelling them. But I didn't mind because all the while, I would fill up on those delicious pecans. I also knew that a pecan pie would be forthcoming very soon and I could hardly wait.

About the end of July the men began talking about deer hunting. That topic always caught my attention because I was full of hope that this year would be the one for my first real deer hunt. I listened to talk of green fields, doe season, rutting season, and guns. It all swirled in my head like eddies circling in the Yazoo River. Then one evening after a few neighbors had gathered for a potluck supper at a neighboring farm, the men's talk turned to speculating about deer stands. For those of you who don't know about them, deer stands are a little like miniature tree-houses but far simpler. They're basically a platform attached to a tall, sturdy tree where a hunter can perch to watch for deer moving about. Tree-stands provide the advantage of keeping your scent above the deer so you will not be detected (unless a hunter is dumb enough to grab a smoke while waiting up there). The hunter gets a better view of what's moving around down below and the deer are not alerted by big feet moving around on the forest floor. But in a tree- stand, caution is paramount. Many a hunter has fallen from them to his death or to life in a wheelchair, usually after falling asleep while waiting in the early morning hours for a deer to pass by.

A new family moved into Greenwood earlier that year. They had come from Arkansas when the father had been transferred here to replace the retiring bank manager at Commerce National Bank. They had a boy my age named Josiah

Dilotush. A new boy in a small town has a hard time, especially if his accent does not blend with the local southern drawl. And red hair and freckles didn't make his life any easier in this land of mostly dark hair and summer tans. But this boy was easy going, quick to smile and slow to anger. I liked him. We soon became friends and I quickly dispensed with his somewhat cumbersome name, nicknaming him Dilo. It stuck immediately and so did we.

Dilo liked to hunt and fish as much as I did and was quick to learn his way around the area, its waterways and its woods. We had a grand time that year doing all the things that high school age boys did back then. After a hard rain, we'd get into my car and go "mud busting". In our part of Mississippi the soil is heavy with clay, and when saturated by rain, the farm fields would be full of mud mounds. I'd drive along the crop rows swerving and spinning around over and through those mounds to break them up.

More often than not, the car would get stuck in the clay based mud. Dilo would get out to push the car as I tried to steer it to firmer ground. But Mississippi mud is hard to deal with because it sticks to anything that touches it. The problem doesn't stop there though. The mud seems to have a mind of its own. Once a boot steps onto its mire, it grabs hold and sucks the boot and its wearer down into the muck. When Dilo would be pushing the car, he'd have a pound of mud on his boots and be barely able to maneuver himself. Quite often he'd wind up on his backside in the mud getting a face full of the mess from the spinning tires. The fun really would start when I'd get out to help him back to his feet. We usually both wound up on the ground in a muddy, whooping free-for-all. We'd often have to ride back to the house with our muddy clothes and boots on the hood of the car. Many's the day that saw us hosing down clothing, boots and our near naked selves out by the barn before we even started cleaning up the filthy car...but it was some kind of fun!

As the temperatures began to moderate and fall was in the air, deer hunting became top on the list of plans and conversations among the hunters around Greenwood. I finally asked my dad if I would get to hunt along with him this year. "I've been waiting on you to ask me that. I figured that when you were ready, you'd ask me about it. So yes Ron, this year you're going with me." I had to work hard to keep my cool when I responded, "Well good. I'm ready...thanks." As you might expect, I gave myself away because two strides outside the back door I was leaping about, flailing my arms and yelling, "Oh yeah! Oh yeah! I'm gonna get myself a big ole buck with a rack a mile wide!" That fourteen year old boy had totally lost his cool. Father and I still laugh about that day even now.

My target practice and gun cleaning began in earnest that very day. It was hard to think of anything else. The teachers at school must have been awfully patient and understanding because they most often got glazed expressions and few answers to their questions from most of the boys in my class over the next four weeks before opening day of deer season. Our minds were seeing little more than the quick flash of the white flag tail of the deer scampering into our gun sights.

After what felt like forever, opening day was almost here. The day before my first hunt I cleaned my gun (yet again) and laid out my clothes, boots, cap, and ammunition. I made sure my trusty Barlow pocket knife was sharp and in the pocket of my hunting pants. I crept around in the woods looking for deer tracks, I watched the green-fields hoping to get a glimpse of deer feeding, I checked out the closest of our tree stands, and I waited. I didn't eat a lot that day. My belly was too full of butterflies and anticipation to hold much else. I was sure I wouldn't be able to sleep that night when I went up to bed and was astonished to hear my dad say, "You better get up and get a move on Ron if you're going hunting with me." I was out of my bed in a flash, dressed and at the kitchen table in a wink. "Guess you better start drinking coffee today, Son. You need to be sharp eyed and not get sleepy on me." Saying that, he poured my first real cup of coffee. When that first gulp of his strong brew hit my stomach, it bounced shockwaves to my brain, mixed with the adrenaline already pumping through my excited nervous system and I was ready to conquer any beast walking.

No one else joined Father and me that day. It was only the two of us. I realize now that my first hunt was as important to him as it was to me. We didn't go to the stand that day, choosing to hunt on foot instead. It was still dark when we set out that morning. We took the farm truck to the edge of the woodlands and then went into the deep woods behind the farm on foot. We went about a mile in before we started looking for our spot to nestle in and wait. We stayed to the eastern side of the travel path the deer followed through that area and above the water source where the path ended. That way we'd be more in darkness and shadows and looking toward the west where the first light of daybreak would show on the deer's' path.

After about half an hour I heard some slight rustling up the path and then silence. Soon I heard a faint sound like the snap of a tiny twig. I glanced up at Father and he gave a brief nod of his head. I raised my gun to my shoulder and waited, breathing as quietly as I could. Then a small yearling doe came into view. Oh, the disappointment! I knew this animal was too young to shoot even if it had been doe season which it wasn't yet. Lowering my gun, I shifted just a bit making enough noise to send that beautiful young lady bounding through the underbrush. I was embarrassed by my mistake in making so much noise, but Father gave a little smile that let me know I'd done no real harm. It was probably another ten or fifteen minutes before my next chance to get my first deer came along. This one came boldly down the path, not as wary as the yearling had been. To my fourteen year old eyes, he was huge. Six points on his antlers told me he was fair game and more. Again I raised my gun, leveled the barrel, put my finger loosely on the trigger and waited. He stepped into a small clearing, stopped to whiff the air, and I did it! I sighted down the barrel, picked that sweet spot just behind his shoulder and gently squeezed the trigger. The deer fell while the shot was still ringing in my ears...no snorting, no thrashing around...a clean shot.

I was dumbstruck for a moment. All the teaching from my dad, all the practice, all the waiting had finally paid off. I'd done it! "Ron that was a perfect shot. Don't think I could have done better myself!" I thought for a moment my father's voice was a little choked but then forgot about it as the realization of the moment hit me full force. I hurried over to check out my kill but slowed before I reached it remembering the warnings drilled into me by Father about the damage that could be inflicted by the sharp antlers of a stunned deer that suddenly regained consciousness. But not this time. I was close enough to see the rivulet of blood oozing from the entrance wound. This deer was as dead as a doornail. I had just captured my first set of antlers to hang on my bedroom wall...or if I was real lucky, over the fireplace in the den and we would put over a hundred pounds of venison into the family freezer. Soon after my deer was field dressed, I also learned what a job carrying that much meat out of the woods can be.

I got two more deer before the season ended and was not bashful about voicing my bragging rights. But I didn't kill every deer I spotted...or thought I spotted. One morning, hunting alone, I left out early heading north of Greenwood on Money Road on public land bordering the Tallahatchie River where lay open fields, a few crops and the ever-present cypress trees in the occasional swampy area. There was heavy dew creating a thick, eerie mist that swirled around my legs as I walked into the woods. The haze blurred the lines of trees and underbrush. I came upon a cypress tree with a hollowed out trunk. I slipped inside it to wait for deer to pass. It was then that I spotted the faint outline of what looked like a gray deer some distance off. It was big, powerful and moving quickly and in the hazy half-light, I was almost convinced my eyes were deceiving me. Deer in our area were brown, not gray. Had I really seen it, or was it just a trick of my imagination? My heart was banging against my chest and blood pulsing in my ears. What was that ghostly apparition? I kept watching for a long time, but it did not reappear. To this day, I don't know if I saw a gray deer or only fell prey to my vivid fourteen year old imagination. I do know that same vision still visits me in dreams now and again. A couple years later I would remember that hollowed out tree, and it would be part of both my undoing and my salvation.

Later on during that winter, the weather turned extremely cold. Not all southern winters are harsh, not like those in the northern parts of the United States. But this winter was one for the record books. But I was a big, tough man now and wouldn't be put off by a cold snap. No, I saw it as the perfect challenge to go duck hunting. Since Dilo had grown up in the Ozark Mountains in Arkansas, our cold spell in Mississippi didn't faze him at all. So off we went. This particular day we took Dilo's old junker Pontiac. He had another car he spent his time and spare money on to keep it in top condition for drag racing...the dangerous, illegal, dare-devil sport of our time. I would help with the tinkerings, tune-ups and mechanical changes that ensured the car's top performance and speed. I never raced myself, having been strictly forbidden to by my parents, but I was always out on those late night runs to cheer him on.

Dilo had recently been having trouble with the Pontiac battery, and on that cold morning of the duck hunt, the engine barely turned over. It did start though, and after loading our gear and ourselves into the car we were underway. We drove to the lake we'd chosen and discovered that it was rimmed in ice. We got into our chest waders, gathered the duck decoys and calls and picked up our guns. I was using a Remington Wingmaster 12 gauge pump shotgun and Dilo a semi-automatic 12 gauge. We began breaking through the ice in a wooded area of the lake to reach open water to put out the decoys. The wind was blowing and cut through us like a knife. By the time we had the decoys set, light was breaking on the horizon.

We could see ducks flying in V formations. We began calling them in, but the ducks would not come in close enough for a shot. Dilo decided to go further out to more open water. I heard him shooting and then he began hollering. I didn't know what was going on but I heard excitement in his voice. While trying to hurry out to him, I tripped on some underwater branches and fell into the water. What a shock of cold I felt as the water seeped inside my waders. When I finally reached

Dilo, I saw he'd shot a Canadian goose. In his excitement, he'd tripped on an underwater log and fell under water. He was soaked with the icy lake water as was his gun. Of course, just then flocks of ducks began coming in, and Dilo's gun would not shoot from freezing up. I reminded him that "...if you had a pump action shotgun like mine, you wouldn't be in this fix." My gun was firing fine. I shot some of the ducks flying in on our calls, but then my shotgun began freezing up as well. Our guns were frozen, we were wet and freezing and needed to get warm so we headed back toward land. When we got back to our decoys, they were frozen in the shallow water. We had to break the ice around them to free them and then stumble on breaking through the surface ice on the lake rim to get to the car. Because we feared frostbite and hypothermia, we decided to get out of our wet clothes before getting into the car. When I attempted to take off my hunting vest, the button holes were frozen and I had a time getting the vest unbuttoned. When I took it off, it stood up on its own like it was made of something solid rather than canvas. When we got down to our long-johns, we jumped into the car praying it would start. Dilo turned the key in the ignition and it gave a weak growl. We were already shivering and shaking from the cold, but that sound didn't help any either. Finally the motor turned over, gave a couple of coughs and began running. Boy was that ever a welcome sound! After a few minutes the car had warmed up enough to turn on the heater. We warmed up a little, and Dilo stopped shaking enough to drive. We needed to get home fast. We needed warm, dry clothes and even more important to clean the ducks for a good hot meal from mom.

Winter turned into an early spring almost overnight. School kept me busy as the workload increased getting all us students ready for the big leap into high school next fall. Basketball gave way to baseball, and when the last sweaty game of the season had been played, I was already knee deep into another growing season at Carrington Farm.

Chapter 5

The summer stretched on hot and humid as only those living in the Delta can understand. It's a kind of heat that leaves not quite enough air to breath. The verdant fields of cotton, corn and soybeans pour oxygen into the air faster than a blacksnake crossing an asphalt road in July, but it's as if the oxygen molecules are instantly surrounded by steam so that when you inhale, half of what you get is water. By the first week of August, I could envision someone holding me by my head and someone else holding my feet and wringing me out like a sheet fresh out of a washtub. But the work required on a farm is no respecter of comfort for those toiling from daylight to sunset to ensure a good harvest. We worked outside every day while the heat waves shimmered in the sweltering air. The only times of respite came when there were thunderstorms with lightning striking all around. And even during those storms there always seemed to be chores inside the barn or house to keep me busy. There was never enough free time for this boy, I can assure you. However, we never worked on Sunday. The Sabbath was strictly observed in our household. Meals were prepared and cleaned up and the livestock seen to, but little else was done in the way of work. I can still hear my Mammaw saying to one of my aunts who had picked up her basket of mending on a quiet Sunday afternoon, "Marie, put that down! Every stitch you sew on Sunday, you'll have to rip out with your nose on Judgment Day!" No, we did not work on Sundays in the Carrington home.

Dilo and I shared a love for frog legs. When battered, floured and fried, they are delicious. Dilo and I found getting them almost as enjoyable as eating them. In our part of the world, most frogs are caught by gigging them. A frog gig reminds me of the pitchfork carried by little red devils with horns and forked tails I've seen in cartoon drawings. I didn't have a gig, but Dilo did. However, the gig Dilo owned had a very long handle. That was a problem because the lightweight flat-bottomed boat we used to hunt the frogs was pretty short, in fact, the gig was longer than the boat. So I found it easier to catch the frogs by hand. Two teenage boys, a gig with wickedly sharp tines and a very short boat were a recipe for disaster and I knew it.

I particularly remember one frog gigging adventure Dilo and I had. It was shortly after I'd turned sixteen because I already had my first car, a Toyota Corona Mark IV. I was so proud of that car and it was my "everything" ride. My dad had bought it for me, but I had to pay for gas and maintenance on it. It was a used car and the paint was not the best but I didn't care. I used cans of green and brown spray paint and turned it into a camouflage beauty.

Dilo called me late one afternoon, "Hey Man, you wanna go get some frogs tonight?" "Hold on a minute and let me see if it's OK with the folks." I found Mother and asked if I could go frogging with Dilo. "It's fine with me, Son..." she said, "but you'd better check with your dad." I went back to the phone and told Dilo I'd call him right back and headed out to the barn. "Hi, Mother said I should check with you to see if I can go after some frogs with Dilo tonight." My father agreed adding a warning, "There won't be much moon tonight. If you boys are going to the canal, be sure you take a gun. The cottonmouths are really bad down there this year." I nodded saying, "Yes sir, they are. Thanks." I went back inside to call Dilo and set the meeting time for 9:30 pm. I knew by then supper would be over, the evening chores done, and I'd be back from taking Alma home. She'd been working late these last couple of weeks because there was so much canning to do since the vegetable garden seemed to be producing at twice its normal rate.

It was about an hour before dinner time, so I went up to my room to get in a little reading. I was and still am a big fan of Louis L 'Amour and was well into "Ride the Dark Trail: The Sacketts". I'd collected several of the books in this series. After about a half hour I heard my dad come inside and settle down with the newspaper. "Ronald, dinner's ready," my mother called. I went to wash up and started downstairs as she called to Father, "Herston, time to eat. Alma's putting the food on the table." "That's right, come on you Carrington men, ya'll eat while everything's hot..." Alma chimed in "...and let me know if you need anything else." We settled around the dining table with Father at the head. As he did at every meal, Father said the blessing. During the meal we enjoyed not only the delicious food but family conversation too. Alma had made a pecan pie earlier in the day, my personal favorite, so the meal ended on a sweet note for me. As was often the case, that night I went into the kitchen to sit with Alma while she ate. She wouldn't eat until after we did. But I liked to sit with her during her meal. It was our time together and she would tell me stories from her childhood, often funny and somehow always wise.

"Dilo and I are going after some frogs tonight, Alma," I told her. "We're taking his boat to the canal." She grinned and said, "Well make sure you get a big mess of 'em. It takes a heap of frog legs to feed you boys!" "Don't we always?" I asked with the confidence only sixteen year olds have. She smiled again and gave my shoulder a pat, "You just be careful, frogs or no frogs." After a few more minutes of clearing up the kitchen, Alma was ready to go home. "I'm taking Alma home then going on over to Dilo's," I called out to my parents.

"Sleep tight and dream about eating frog legs," I quipped.

I arrived at Dilo's a little after nine. We loaded his boat into the back of his truck and then the gear from my car. I'd brought along my Marlin .22 semi-automatic rifle and about 250 rounds of ammo for the snakes. We set out for the spot we liked to put in on the canal. When we got there we took the boat out of the truck at the edge of the canal. Dilo then raised the hood of the truck to unhook the battery cables because he used the same battery to power the spotlight we used to "shine on" the frogs. "Dilo, why don't you get a battery just for the spotlight? One of these nights we're going to use up all the battery power and then not be able to get the truck started!" Easy going Dilo shrugged his shoulders and said, "Naw, we'll have plenty of juice for both. You're not up for a little adventure?" Not wanting to come across as a sissy, I answered, "Hey, no problem here, man. Let's get going." I will admit part of me was a little uneasy but a bigger part was full of bravado and enjoyed flirting with the possibility of trouble.

It was pitch black along the canal and the hot air so close and sticky that sweat was rolling off both of us by the time we'd hauled the two and one-half horsepower motor from the truck and clamped it onto the back of the boat. We sprayed down with insect repellent which seemed to be little more than an aerosol appetizer for the cloud of vampire mosquitoes that surrounded us. More often than not we got more protection from those hungry biters by smearing ourselves with mud. So off we went with our little motor on our little short boat, in the black of night, in an eight foot wide snaky canal on a quest to find and capture a gastronomic delight...frogs, lots and lots of frogs.

Since I did not like using Dilo's gig, or any gig for that matter, we had devised a very workable system. Dilo sat in the back of the boat and steered while I sat up in the front of the boat. By shining the spotlight along the canal bank, I'd see the frogs when the light reflected off their eyes. I'd hand the light to Dilo as he steered closer to them. I would lean over the front of the boat before it touched the bank and grab them as they stared wide-eyed into the light. Then into a big plastic bag the frogs went. If the boat hit the bank too soon, the frogs jumped into the water and were gone, so ours was a method of either precise timing and accuracy or failure. And as I think back on it now, I'm somewhat amazed that two age-awkward sixteen year old boys ate as many frog legs as we did.

As my dad had warned earlier, we saw far more snakes than usual that night. True cottonmouth moccasins are not pleasant creatures. They are thin bodied, malodorous things with ill tempers and deadly venomous bites. They often lay along low-hanging tree limbs around water.

I remembered that about them when we spotted some frogs along the canal bank under a tree. "Dilo, slow way down so I can shake those tree branches with the boat paddle in case there are snakes on them." I wished at that moment for Dilo's frog gig with the too long handle for this job. But the paddle was all I had. I pushed it against the tree branch and began to shake it. Sure enough a snake was in the tree and fell...unfortunately, into the boat. Dilo was scrambling to get as far back and away from the snake as he could, all the while yelling, "Shoot it Ron! Shoot the snake!" I yelled back, "I can't shoot it. I'll put a hole in the boat and it'll sink!" I also knew we couldn't jump out because there were more snakes outside the boat than in it. I grabbed the paddle again and started trying to flip the snake over the side of the boat and back into the canal water. Finally I got it out, but barely. Because of the weight of two boys, a truck battery, and a sack of frogs, the boat was riding so low in the water there was only about an inch of space between the boat lip and the top of the water. As we headed down the canal that snake swam right alongside of us. It seemed he was half in and half out of the boat with each S curve of his undulating body. "What is it with this crazy snake !?!" Dilo hollered. "He's mad as the devil!" I yelled back, "I can't get a good shot at him because he's too close to the boat. Rev up that engine and let's get out of here!" Dilo opened it up and we were able to get away from the snake. "That was close, Dilo. No more frogs under trees tonight!" "I'm with you on that!" he agreed. We meandered on up the canal bagging several more frogs along the way and shooting more snakes than you can shake a stick at. I checked my ammo can and told Dilo, "I'm running low on bullets, but we still need a few more frogs." "Better save them only for the big snakes," he answered. I agreed with that thinking. We frog hunted a little longer and grabbed a few more when I spotted a frog that looked like a sure catch. We approached the bank and just as I was reaching out to grab it I saw a huge moccasin eyeing that same frog with a hungry look. I snatched my hand back and told Dilo, "Back us out of here as quick as you can! The biggest snake I've seen tonight had his eye on that frog. If I'd grabbed for that frog, I'd have got bit for sure! I don't know about you, but I've had enough of fighting with snakes over frogs for one night." Dilo grinned and started maneuvering the boat around to head back toward the truck. "This was some night, Ron," Dilo said. "You're right about that" I answered. "I've never seen more snakes in my life and," I added, "we've never caught more frogs in one night either!" We arrived back to our original location without any problems, loaded the boat onto the truck along with the gun, the frogs and other gear. Then it was time to hook the trusty old battery back up to the truck engine. Luck and the Good Lord were with us yet again. When Dilo cranked the truck, the engine turned over and we were headed home...hot, tired and relieved. We finally made it home about 2:00 am and had the frogs cleaned and divided between the two of us in an hour. As I climbed the stairs and headed for a shower and then bed, it was in anticipation of a delicious meal come tomorrow.

When I got up the next morning, I showed the frog legs to my mom. "Alma and I will fry them up this evening for us," she said, "They'll make a fine dinner tonight, Son." I smiled, "Thanks Mom, I can taste them now!" I called Dilo to check in on him.

"Did you get home OK last night?" "Yep, no problems. Boy what a night! That was so much fun," Dilo answered. "Well good eatin' tonight, Dilo. Talk to you later," I said as I hung up.

When Alma saw all the frog legs I'd brought home, she started laughing. "What's so funny, Alma?" I asked. "Oh I was just picturing how much jumping those legs are going to do when they hit that frying pan full of hot oil tonight," she answered. "Reminds me of how you always jumped around the room when you'd be in trouble when you were a little thing. I'd be after you with a switch and you'd leap around all over the place trying to get away from me. You'd even be up on the furniture going from tables to chairs to, well, just any place you could get. I don't know if you were more like a frog or a monkey, but you sure led me on some chases!" I was laughing along with her remembering those days and commented, "We usually got so tickled that we both wound up laughing our heads off and you forgot about whipping me!"

Chapter 6

Labor Day of 1976 was drawing near. That was always a wonderful day at Carrington Farm every year. My folks hosted a big barbeque picnic for friends, relatives and neighbors from miles around. Preparations for it began weeks in advance. Mother and Alma would cook and freeze casseroles and vegetables. My father would be choosing the hog that would slowly spin on the spit over the open fire pit. It took at least 24 hours for the meat to be done and ready to eat. He had several men who helped in the cooking process, but he kept a watchful eye all the same.

The day prior to the gathering was the day for dessert making...pies, cakes, fruit salads...delights to only be dreamed of. All men (and boys) were banned from the kitchen on that day. Father and I were on our own, but we didn't mind. Sometimes it's better not to be around when the women of the house are in a cooking frenzy.

Early on the morning of Labor Day, tables and benches were set up in the front and side yards around our house. We had four sets of our own and the rest were brought in by neighbors. Each table could seat ten to twelve people depending on how closely together they sat, and the children would all sit at separate tables leaving the adults to their own "boring" conversation.

Guests would begin arriving around 11:00 am to visit and help out if needed. We always hoped for good weather on those Labor Days so the music and games could be enjoyed with free abandon. Fiddlers and guitar pickers were in great supply among those in our community and my father and a couple of the other men would roll mother's spinet piano out onto the front porch. Voices would join together in old favorites as well as hymns and spirituals praising God who had given a good harvest and abundance to our lives. Sometimes the younger musicians among us would strike out into the rock music of the time, but that usually was stopped pretty quickly when we younger ones started to dance. Not everyone, but many of our gathered friends frowned on such shenanigans.

By mid-afternoon, the smell of that roasting pig would be redolent in the air. Hickory smoke, sizzling pork, fresh cut fields and sumptuous food mingled together in a heady fragrance that would have even the most peevish of the figure conscious among us salivating in anticipation of the meal to come. Cold lemonade and sweet iced tea disappeared by the gallons as did stolen nibbles from the food laden tables. At 3:00 pm sharp my dad would stand on the front porch and ring the wrought iron triangle dinner bell for gathering the crowd. He'd remove his ever-present hat and bow his head as he announced the time for prayer. As he did each year at this event, Father began his prayer by quoting from the Bible, the Book of Psalms, chapter 128:1-2: "Blessed is everyone that loves the Lord and walks in His ways. For thou shalt eat the labor of thine hands: happy shalt thou be, and it shall be well with thee."

After grace had been said, the feast began...and a feast it truly was. Food, prepared by Mother and Alma, was added to from households from every corner of our community. Every cook around, men and women alike, brought their very best creations. This was the peak of the casserole era started by the Campbell Soup company a few years back. It was joked that no Baptist church in the south could have a supper if casserole recipes weren't on the back of Campbell soup cans. There was no shortage of them on Labor Day of 1976 I can assure you. There was also a party and picnic drink known as Baptist Punch that always showed up at these gatherings. Mother didn't make it, but Miss Minnie Stillwell, the local sheriff's mother did. It was a mixture of lime jello, pineapple juice and 7-Up. It was so sweet it would knock your head off, but many liked it. Miss Minnie floated an ice cube with a cherry inside of it in each serving. The little children scrambled for it just to get one of those ice cubes. Many a young hand got smacked for trying to fish around in the punch bowl to snatch out one of those precious ice cubes. For that reason (along with all the sticky sweetness) I steered away from that beverage...too many messy little fingers in the drink did not suit my taste.

After the meal was finished the adults would settle down for conversation and digestion, but the children would continue their play. My friends and I would wander off away from the others for our own kind of fun. We'd laugh and talk about all the things we were interested in, boys and girls would giggle and flirt and we'd pass the time until dusk when our favorite games could get underway. We always played "Starlight, Starbright, Hope I See A Ghost Tonight". We'd choose someone to be the Ghost. That person would then hide somewhere around the house while everyone else kept their eyes shut. After the count of 100, we'd spread out from the front steps which was home base. As we walked around the perimeter of the house, The Ghost would jump out and tag a passer-by. That person would then become a ghost too. When the ghost revealed himself, everyone else would holler out and try to run around the house back to home base before being tagged. All who were tagged before reaching home base would become ghosts, and round two of the game would begin. As the game wore on, the number of ghosts grew so that by the third or fourth round, ones chances of getting all the way around the house without being tagged were quite slim. Between the darkness and the unknown hiding places of the many ghosts, it was scary business trying to make it around our big house. Lots of shrieks sounded out in the night from those who failed.

We had another game call "Kick The Can". In it everyone except the "It" hid in the yard. "It" stood inside a circle drawn on the ground with an empty can at the center of the circle. After everyone had hidden, the person inside the circle went out in search of the others who were hidden. When the "It" saw someone, "It" would run back to the circle and holler, "1,2,3, I see you hiding at so and so place." The circle would get filled up with kids who had been identified. If the "It" ventured far enough away from the circle, one of the players hiding could make a run for the circle to kick the can as far outside the circle as possible. If that happened, then everyone in the circle would become free and could run and hide again until the can was placed back in the center of the circle by "It".

If everyone got caught, then the first one to get caught would then be "It" and the game would begin again. These were fun times that I remember with great fondness.

By nine or ten on those nights, eyelids were getting heavy and people started packing up and heading for home. The cooks would have already covered the fire pit and put everything away.

Leftover food, what little there was, was divided among the families to be taken home to enjoy another day. Tables and lawn chairs were packed away and everything was put back in place. Another Labor Day picnic at Carrington Farm would draw to a close with warm wishes and loving good-byes. This was always a peaceful time, but this year it was not to be so.

Chapter 7

With the last of the guests gone, my exhausted parents headed into the house and their comfortable beds. I called out my good-nights to them thanking them for another great day. "You coming in soon, Son?" asked Mother. "Yes, ma'am...pretty soon. I want to enjoy some of this quiet and watch the stars a little while," I answered. I lay down on the soft grass gazing into the heavens, picking out constellations. Before long my fatigue began to catch up with me and I was in a near-dream state when I heard a whisper. "Quick, get him!" growled a voice I didn't recognize. In a flash someone grabbed my wrists and another hand stuffed a gag into my mouth. A funny smelling cloth was clamped over my nose, and everything went black. The next thing I remember was being aware that my hands and feet were bound. I was quite groggy and had no idea where I was or what was going on. I did sense that I was in a moving vehicle, and since I was face down on the floorboard, I could not see what type vehicle. Something was pressing into my back and it hurt. I turned my head to the side enough to see two men sitting on the back seat of the car holding me down with their feet. I must have moaned from the pain because one of them yelled, "Shut up kid!" He dug his heel into my ribs. I'm sure I must have groaned again but then was silent. I heard one of the men say, "Just be sure you keep him quiet or I'll have to chloroform the little punk again!"

It was so dark in the car I could not make out their faces, and I didn't recognize their voices. I did notice they had peculiar accents though. They sounded vaguely like Dilo with his Arkansas mountain twang. I thought to myself, what in the world is going on? Who are these men? What do they want with me? As the realization hit me that I could be in real danger, I shivered in fear.

We seemed to be hurtling down the road at a fast clip. "Hey Harry, slow down," said someone in the front seat, "the last thing we need is to get pulled over for speeding by some local yokel!" A much deeper voice answered, "Who's driving this durned car?" But the car slowed a little.

I then knew there were four men in the car with me. It frightened me even more to know I had so many to contend with. I was trying to clear my head, calm down and think clearly when we hit a big pothole. The car bounced hard and the four heavy feet on my back dug in deep. I screamed out and got an even harder kick, "I told you to shut up!" I fought back tears of pain and fear. "Why are these men doing this to me and what do they want?" I was absolutely terrified.

The car slowed and turned. I could tell we were going up a slight incline, then we went over two big bumps and then started heading down again. It seemed like we'd gone over a railroad track. "Harry! Watch the mud! We don't want to get stuck," said the man in the front passenger seat. "OK, OK I know what I'm doing," came the grouchy reply. We went on slowly a little further then stopped. "All out...quick!" said the driver. The two men in the back seat got out of the car. One of them grabbed me by my legs and pulled me across the floorboard and onto the ground. I could feel the rough floorboard lining scraping my face before I smacked face down onto the ground. I turned my face to the side and held it up as he pulled me further along. He dropped my legs and left me laying there when one of the men said, "Get the car unloaded quick. Stan, you and Mike start getting brush to cover up the car. It needs to be camouflaged so it can't be seen." Then he barked another order, "Harry, go make sure all the tire tracks are stomped out of the mud where we turned in off the highway and make it quick." I heard the driver say, "Sure Doug, we know what to do." Doug hissed a curt, "Just hurry and do your jobs!" The moon was nearly full that night and slivers of light shone through the heavy tree limbs above me. I was able to get quick glimpses of my four captors.

Doug seemed to be the one in charge. He appeared to be fortyish with dark hair and small, beady eyes. He was more slightly built than the others and moved in quick, jerky motions. He reminded me of a rat somehow. He had a short stubbly beard and no apparent smile. He seemed very nervous. The driver, Harry, had thick black hair that looked greasy and unkempt. His arms were beefy, but he sported a big pot belly. Mike and Stan who had been in the backseat holding me down were younger. They had long, straggly hair, and it was apparent they were very muscular. Mike, the man who had stomped on my back so hard, was missing a front tooth. Usually I was not too keen about remembering such characteristics of people and I surprised myself with how minutely I studied each of the assailants. Their images were burned into my brain. I think the sheer terror of this experience had my adrenalin pumping through my body so fast that my brain was processing in high gear. I was on high alert. I'd had similar feelings before on hunting trips, but nothing like this.

Doug began snapping out orders to the other men. "Harry, you backtrack to the train tracks and stand watch and make sure no one is following us while the other guys finish covering the car." "Sure Doug, but I don't think anyone will be out here this time of night," Harry replied. "You're not here to think! Just do what I said!" Doug spit back. Harry walked toward the edge of the woods while Mike and Stan continued covering the car with tree limbs and brush.

I was able to get the gag out of my mouth with my tied hands. "What's going on? What do you want with me?" I yelled out. Mike kicked me in the face, and I thought I was going to pass out as my stomach lurched from nausea. "I told you to keep quiet kid!" he bellowed. Doug hissed at Mike, "Don't knock him out you idiot or you'll be carrying him to camp over your shoulder."

Doug walked over to me then and addressed me directly for the first time, "You'll know soon enough, and until then you'd best keep that yap shut or you'll get hurt real bad." His eyes were as flat and cold as the tone of his voice and I somehow knew he meant exactly what he said. I stared at him not daring to say a word while he stuffed the gag back into my mouth. Stan walked over to where I lay to tell Doug the car was covered. "Are you sure no light will reflect off it come morning?" Doug questioned. "Yup, I'm sure," Stan said. "Ok, go get Harry and let's get going," Doug ordered.

Stan went and got Harry while Mike used his switchblade knife to cut the ropes tying my legs.

He grabbed me by my arms pulling me to my feet. All four men grabbed backpacks they had brought in the car. Mike told me, "follow Doug" and the others followed behind me. We set out through the woods following a trail marked with little orange flags that I assumed they'd placed before my capture. After walking what I guessed to be a mile, we reached a clearing where a camp had been set up. There was wood piled by a fire ring, a tent and four chairs. To the side of the fire ring was a cooler and some bags. "Ok, let's get the kid tied up," said Doug, leading me to a tree on the edge of the campsite. Mike picked up a length of rope motioning for me to sit at the base of the tree. He wrapped the rope three or four times around my chest and the tree, tying the knot on the opposite side of the tree from me. My hands were still tied in my lap. The bark of the pine tree cut into my back and hurt. The rope was made of cotton and would stretch slightly so Mike pulled it extra tight.

Chapter 8

The gang, as I had begun to think of them, settled in for the night. With Doug cautioning him to keep it low, Mike built a fire. They all got beers out of the cooler and settled into their chairs around the fire. "Well boys, I think we pulled it off just fine," Doug bragged. "Harry, you left the ransom note on the porch like I said, right?" "Sure did, Doug," Harry answered, "In plain view just like you said, with the flower pot holding it down and on the first step. They'll be sure to see it come morning when their boy don't show for breakfast." So that was it, they wanted to trade me for money!

They drank their beer in silence for a while. "What're you gonna do with your part of the money Doug?" asked Harry. Doug smiled for the first time, "I'm going to the Bahamas, lay on the beach all day while beautiful girls bring me drinks...you know, the ones with the little umbrellas in 'em." Harry then asked Mike, "What about you Cuz?" Mike didn't have to think for a minute before he answered,"I'm going on up north and open me up a bar. I'm gonna sit 'n drink all day 'n watch the money rollin' in," he laughed. Stan blurted out, "I'm taking off for Mexico. I hear it's real cheap to live there. I'll have a big house full of servants at my beck and call night and day."

Then Harry piped in, "Well I'm not goin' back to Arkansas. That's for sure! Think I'll go overseas, maybe live in Paris for a while, take in the sights, and see those dancing girls I've heard about. Then I might move on to Italy. Hear they have some pretty good food there, and I can go to that place with all those canals all over the town. I'll ride around in one of those funny looking boats." "We can do all the dreaming after the money's in our hands," Doug said. "For now, let's eat and get some sleep. Stan, you take first watch." After they ate, Doug said to Mike, "Give the kid a drink of water. We don't want him to croak before we get the cash."

The camp area was pretty small and obviously it was recently formed. It was, I decided, a temporary thing purely for the time required for my parents to pay the ransom demanded for my return. As I thought about that, I began to wonder why the gang did not blindfold me or hide their identities. When the realization hit me, my blood turned to ice. There was no plan to return me to my parents at all. I was as good as dead from the minute I was captured. If they had planned on returning me, the kidnappers would have never let me see their faces or hear their plans for the future. I'd heard them talk about it all, and wouldn't they know I would give that information to the authorities? Oh it was so clear now. It did not matter what I saw or heard because it wouldn't matter if I was not alive to tell anyone.

Mike ambled over to me and yanked the gag from my mouth. He poured a sip of water through my lips and said, "You want to know what's goin' on, boy? Seems we've snatched you away from mommy and daddy, and now you're gonna get us a million dollars. We heard all about you from the kin of that Dilotush boy you're so friendly with. Seems he went on and on about you and your rich family when he was back up for that visit this summer. You rich people got all the money and now we're getting ours." Then he slapped me across the mouth. In a stunned state I asked, "Why are you being so mean to me? I haven't done anything to you!" Mike stood up kicking me hard in the leg, "Shut up your smart mouth you little brat!" he screamed. Pain was shooting through my bleeding mouth and my leg, and I broke down sobbing. "Oh you poor little rich kid," Mike teased. "Your kind gets everything and I get nothing!" Mike was shouting again and was about to pummel me when Doug stepped between us, "Calm down Mike. We don't need to make mistakes now. We need him for a while longer, so just back off!"

Doug turned to Stan saying, "Let's go over this plan one more time. His family has two days to get the money together. When we contact them, tell them that. It says that in the note but be sure they understand...its two days and no more, and they don't call the cops! Tell them you'll let them know where the drop-off spot is the next day. If they ask to exchange the money for him, say no. Tell his old man we'll let him know where he can get the kid after we pick up the money and are gone. Harry, you pick up the money and bring it here, we'll divide it, drive to our getaway point and go our separate ways. Every one of you make sure you follow the plan. No slip-ups! No mistakes!" Stan said, "Alright Doug! We've been over this a hundred times already!" Then Harry made the chilling comment, "We never decided who'd take care of the boy after the pick-up." Doug turned away saying, "You let me worry about that." That's when Mike spoke up, "I'm willing to pay for the privilege of taking out the rich little twerp. I'd give ten grand for that!" Doug asked, "Does anyone else want to pay more for him?" None of the others spoke up, so Doug turned to Mike and said, "For ten grand, he's all yours. Just be sure you do it right." Mike turned and looked at me with a wicked grin and hate filled his eyes.

Chapter 9

The four guys sat and drank a few more beers. They were constantly swatting at the pesky mosquitoes buzzing around them. The blood-thirsty little things were swarming around me too. I kept shaking my head and blowing them away as they whined around my eyes and neck. "Hey rich boy, you want some of this bug spray?" Mike called out as he sprayed a cloud of it around himself. "Yes sir, please," I pleaded. "Listen to that. He said please," Mike taunted. "Too bad you little piece of crap...deal with it," was his hateful reply. Laughing at me in my misery, they all continued guzzling their beer until finally Stan got up and headed to the edge of the clearing and into the woods to stand watch. Doug and Harry headed toward the tent. I heard Harry tell Doug that he'd relieve Stan at guard in three hours. Mike came over and tied one end of a length of rope around my neck. He then tied the other end around his wrist saying, "I wouldn't want to lose you now would I!" He lay down on a sleeping bag about three feet away from me. In a few short minutes he was snoring.

It was a very humid night and the dampness made the ground chilly. I was wishing for the warmth of a sleeping bag for myself. As I sat there thinking about what had happened and even worse of what lay ahead for me, it was hard for me to concentrate. I had no doubts about what they planned to do with me after I was of no further use to them. I was to DIE! I then realized my only hope for staying alive was to keep calm, be logical and pray that God would see me through this. I had no time for self-pity.

I began to assess my situation methodically. I was unclear about where I was, but I did know I was in a wooded area. The dampness of the air and ground along with the over-abundance of mosquitoes let me know that a swap was most likely near-by. I knew I was held by four desperate, evil men capable of murder. I knew they were all armed. I had seen Mike's switchblade. Stan carried a rifle with a scope on it. I'd glimpsed a revolver in the waist-band of Doug's jeans and Harry had used a machete to cut branches for the fire. I was tethered to Mike's wrist so any movement I made would be detected. Only three of them slept at the same time. I knew Stan was on guard. Even though I'd seen the direction he'd gone, I could not see his exact location, but I was sure he was awake. As I pondered my situation I dozed fitfully while the mosquitoes chewed on all my exposed skin and the same question reverberated in my mind, "HOW do I escape these evil men?"

I could get little sleep that night for many reasons, not the least of which was Mike's jerking the rope tied around my neck every time he swatted at the persistent mosquitoes. He finally got so exasperated with the mosquitoes that he untied the rope from around his wrist and went into the tent and its merciful mosquito netting. Doug roused from his alcohol laced sleep to say, "Whatcha doin' in here? That boy might get away you fool!" Harry, also awakened by Mike crowding into the tent, said, "That kid can't go anywhere. His hands and feet are tied, and he's tied to that tree." Doug grumbled back, "Alright then, but if he gets loose, you and Mike will answer to me." With that he turned over and was asleep again. Shortly thereafter, Stan came walking into camp. He pushed his way into the tent waking Harry who snorted, "What's the matter with you? Your watch ain't over yet." A grouchy Stan replied, "I'm tired and itching to death from all these bug bites. Nobody's coming around here tonight! If you want this camp guarded, go do it yourself. I'm getting some sleep."

Even though the bark of the pine tree cut into my back, my thoughts wandered to my warm bed at home. It was at that moment I envisioned what my parents would face come morning. I'd been so engrossed in my own predicament and how to escape, considering my parent's situation had not entered my mind. Oh, the pain and fear that lay ahead for them! I prayed in anguish, "Dear God in Heaven, please hold my family in your arms and calm their fear! Please!"

Chapter 10

"Ron, wake up! Your breakfast will be ready soon. Your momma's going to need your help cleaning up the yard from that bar-b-que yesterday," Alma called up the stairs. After a few minutes of silence, she mused to herself, "Guess I'll have to drag that young man out of his bed myself. I need to get him moving or we're both going to get behind this morning." Alma trudged up the steps thinking to herself how much easier this trip was a few years ago. "Time's not a friend to my tired, old knees," she mused.

Alma was surprised when she went into Ron's room. It was neat and tidy and the bed already made up. "...not like him to do that before he puts food in his belly," she thought. When she got back to the kitchen, Virginia was coming in the back door with Herston. They'd been out for a brisk stroll around the back flower beds while they waited for Ron to come down to breakfast. It was a morning ritual they'd observed for years. "Ron not with you?" Alma asked. "No, haven't seen him," they replied almost in unison. "Well he's up and out somewhere, and you won't believe this, his bed is already made up!" Herston headed for the front of the house calling out to his son. Hearing no response, he went out on the front porch to call for the boy...still no answer. He started down the front steps when he spotted a piece of paper stuck under a flower pot by the first step. Thinking Ron had left a note for them, he casually bent to get it. When his eyes fell to the note, Herston gasped and staggered over to the nearest chair. He read the note again thinking it couldn't be real...but there it was.

If you want to see your boy alive again it will cost you one million dollars. You have two days. We will contact you tonight. CASH! HUNDREDS! NO COPS!!!

Herston was gasping for air, his heart pounding in his chest. Tears flooded his face. He was frozen in place. A wrenching groan escaped his throat as he stood shakily and began walking toward the kitchen. Virginia was already sipping coffee and leafing through the newspaper when Herston stopped in the doorway. Without looking up from her paper, she asked, "Did you find that boy? Breakfast is going to be too cold to eat." When her husband did not answer she looked up and was startled by his ashen, tear-streaked face. "Herston, what's wrong? Are you sick?" Alma, hearing the alarm in Virginia's voice, turned from the sink and saw the piece of paper clenched in Herston's hand. She instinctively moved toward Virginia's chair and was standing behind it when Herston held the note out to his wife. Virginia's scream echoed through the house as she read the hateful message.

Herston caught Virginia before she hit the floor. She lay prostrate in his arms crying out, "Why? Why? What have they done with my baby?" As Herston tried to sooth her, he was feeling a whirlwind of his own emotions...fear, anger, disbelief and even guilt. How could he let something like this happen right under his nose? Why had he not insisted that Ron come inside before he went up to bed last night? Who would do this, and how did they take his son so quietly? "Precious Father, help me get my boy!" he prayed in agony.

Alma sprang into action upon seeing the ransom note. A cool cloth was pressed to Virginia's forehead and a cup of coffee into Herston's hands the minute he had Virginia resting on the chaise on the sun-porch adjoining the kitchen. And all the time she was in motion, Alma was praying to God for mercy and strength for this family and for protection for beloved Ron. While Herston and Virginia were deciding what to do next, Alma slipped to the telephone to call Eustus. She knew he was working for Dr. Miller that day putting in shelving in a storage closet. When the doctor's receptionist answered, Alma asked for Eustus. When he answered she told him there was a need for serious prayer for the Carrington family for private reasons. Eustus asked for no details. He and Alma understood that God knows what the problem is when special prayer is needed. Alma then called the Carrington's pastor with the same request. Upon returning to the sunroom, Alma found the Carrington's in deep discussion. Not wanting to intrude she started from the room when Virginia said, "Did you call Eustus and Pastor Gordon?" Alma shook her head yes. "Thank you, Alma. It's a comfort to have you here."

As Herston set about the task of liquidating funds and setting up account withdrawals to begin amassing the ransom money, Virginia slipped up to Ron's room. She walked around picking up various mementos and trophies from his youth, some of his favorite books, the little John Deere toy tractor that still sat in his windowsill. She lay down on his bed and smelled his teen-aged boy smell. And she prayed.

So many times through the years Virginia talked to her Sunday school girls about faith in God's wisdom and goodness. She'd read to them from the Bible about the strength that comes from God in times of trial. She'd been diligent in teaching them that Christians accept the will of God even if they don't understand it. On this day she was saying those same things to herself. She believed them with her entire being. But her mother's heart still spoke the words of pleading, "Please God, you have three of my babies. Please let it fall within your will to grant this mercy. Keep Ron safe and return him to us. Please don't take my last baby now."

Chapter 11

Daylight would be breaking soon and I would have another day of this torture to endure. My hands and feet were already numb from lack of blood flow because the ropes were so tight. My fingernails were already blue and I knew my feet were just as bad. I needed to get some relief but did not know how I would accomplish it. My health was not important to my captors. I also knew that I'd have to wait for them to wake up before anything might be done. Waking them up myself would only make matters worse.

As I waited for morning, I again assessed my situation. Today my dad would be working on gathering the ransom money. I was not sure how he'd do that. We were very comfortable financially, but I was sure he didn't have one million dollars readily at hand. But I felt sure he'd manage it somehow. The money was to be handed over to my kidnappers tomorrow, so that left me one day and one night to formulate and execute an escape plan. That was a tall order for a seventeen year old boy. Today I must be calm, polite, meek even.

I must do nothing to anger or excite them because they could as easily kill me today as tomorrow. I would watch and wait today, look for any means of escape and make my move later tonight...that is, if I could come up with a plan.

As sunlight hit the tent, Doug sat up complaining, "It's too cramped in here and you guys smell awful. Everybody get out!" Mike retorted, "Keep your shirt on, man! We're going." They all ambled in different directions into the woods to relieve themselves before returning to the campfire. It had died down to a few glowing embers during the night and Stan began adding more wood to it. As the flames licked upward, I could feel the welcome heat warming me a little. Mike came over and checked my ropes, "Just as tight as ever, eh kid?" he snickered. I quietly asked him, "Could I please get untied long enough to go urinate?" He roared with laughter, "Little rich boy wants to take a leak. Too bad! Piss in your pants for all I care." Doug called over, "Let him go into the woods. If he pisses in his pants, then we have to smell it all day." Untying my feet and hands Mike said, "You better make it a good one...it will be the only one you get all day." He then untied me from the tree and I tried to stand up. At first I couldn't feel my feet at all. Then suddenly it was like thousands of needles stabbing my hands and feet both. "Hurry up," Mike shouted. "I can't stand up!" I said. Kicking me in the ribs, Mike yelled, "Then crawl punk!" His kick knocked the wind out of me and I had trouble moving as well as breathing. Harry walked over and gave me a kick in my legs saying, "Get on over there. We ain't waitin' on you all day. What's the matter with you? Can't you do anything right?" Doug came over then and started shoving me with his foot, "Move boy!" I managed to crawl to the edge of the woods and lean against a tree. I was so sore and stiff, I couldn't stand up straight. After relieving myself, I stumbled back to my pine tree and sat down. I asked for water but Mike said, "No water for you today, that way you won't have to worry about taking a piss." Then Mike tied me back up as before and said, "Now keep quiet or I'll put the gag back in your mouth." I nodded my compliance and settled down to watch and wait.

Not long after the four had eaten breakfast, it began drizzling rain. Muttering a string of curses,

Doug headed back into the tent. Stan put some firewood in the tent to keep dry. I heard him say to Doug, "What a miserable place! I don't know why anyone would want to live here." Then Harry chimed in, "Yeah, it'll be great to get out of here tomorrow, especially as rich men!" Doug agreed, "Yeah, I'm ready. His old man should have the money in hand by tomorrow afternoon, we make the pick-up, split the cash and we're outta here." Mike looked over at me and smirked, "And I get my special fun when I off the kid. Still deciding how I'm gonna do it, but it won't be quick and painless. I promise you that. He's gonna cry like a little girl." With that he cackled a wicked laugh that ended in a fit of coughing.

The rain stopped. Stan built up the fire and pulled a package of wieners out of the cooler. The gang cooked their hot dogs over the fire and settled down to eat. Soon I heard the pop of the never-ending cans of beer. Stan went toward the look-out point and the other three started playing poker. "Let's make this interesting, fellas. Each of us will get thirty peanuts each out of this can of nuts, and each one is worth a thousand dollars. We can all settle up with real money tomorrow night," Doug instructed. They played steadily for about three hours when Stan came into camp. "Hey Mike, it's your turn to stand guard." Mike replied, "Fair enough, I already owe Harry twenty grand!" Doug laughingly taunted Mike, "...and don't forget the ten thou you owe me for giving you the boy." Mike jumped up angrily and headed to the guard post. Stan got a beer and sat in on the ongoing game. Another guard shift passed and Mike came in calling Harry to go stand his turn as guard. Stan said to Harry, "That's enough poker for me. I'm down fifteen thousand to you and Doug both." Doug laughed and said, "Fine with me, I'm up twenty-five thousand all together, and anyway, I'm hungry." Mike agreed on both counts. "You want to cook something, Doug?" he asked. "No, let's eat a sandwich for now and not build up the fire until closer to dark." Mike then made the mistake of asking, "When are you standing guard, Doug. You ain't been out there one time." The stinging reply was rapid, "And I won't be! I have to do all the thinking for you bunch of goons, so shut up your whining about it. You'll each do one more guard shift before we call it quits tonight. It'll be close on to midnight, and I doubt anybody's going to be around here after that. Right now, I'm going to make the call to the kid's old man and get this ball rolling. There's a pay phone outside the old gas station just on the outskirts of town.

Chapter 12

It had been a tense, mournful day at Carrington Farm. The minutes crept by for Virginia. She felt so helpless, so alone. Had it not been for the hovering presence of Alma bringing her lemonade, a cup of tea, any morsel of food she could manage to swallow, Virginia didn't know if she could have stopped her silent screams from escaping her lips. But she held on. The near-silent murmuring of prayers from Alma's lips gave Virginia courage and she began to add prayers of her own. Two women bound together over seventeen years for the protection of the child were bound even closer again on this day; for his continued protection...for his life.

For Herston the minutes were whizzing by too fast. Heeding the warning in the ransom note about police involvement, he had contacted no one except his trusted attorney and friend, Ray LaRoche. Ray had been his business associate for over twenty years and his friend even longer. Herston knew that Ray was a man he could trust with Ron's life. Within an hour of his telephoning

Ray, they were ensconced in Herston's study working on the matter of gathering the ransom money. Between them, Herston and Ray had the contacts and clout to make such a huge sum of cash materialize with no questions from those with whom they dealt. Their real enemy was not the amount of money they needed, it was time. Brokerage firms, banks, private lenders all seemed to move at a snail's pace. They were finalizing their last transaction when Herston heard the phone ring. At first he froze, then immediately ran toward the phone. Ray was right on his heels and both men listened intently knowing Ron's life was on the line.

"Hey, is this Carrington?" Doug's voice crackled through the phone. "If you want to see your precious brat again, you'll listen and do what I tell you!" Holding the phone with his hand shaking, Herston answered, "I'm here. Who is this and what have you done with my son?" Doug curtly responded, "You don't worry about who I am! Just listen, old man. Did you get my note?" Herston quickly answered, "I have it and I'm working on getting your money together. Can I speak to my son?" Doug shot back, "Not yet Carrington. Do you have my money ready?" Herston's voice quivered with anger and fear as he answered, "I have over half the money now and the rest is on its way. I swear to you I'll have it in two days' time like the note said." Doug shouted, "You better have all of it by then if you want to see your boy alive again. I'll call back tomorrow and tell you the drop-off spot for the money." Hurling that threat, Doug hung up the phone leaving Herston staring at the phone while tears of anguish and frustration coursed down his weathered face. Turning to Ray, Herston fought for control of his emotions, "We'd better get back at it. That animal means it; he'll kill my son if he doesn't get what he wants."

Chapter 13

Doug returned to the campsite after making the call. It was getting dark when Stan built up the fire to heat up canned beans. The aroma of them made my mouth water. I'd been given no food all day. But I had more important things to think about than my empty belly. Tonight was my only chance to escape. I watched quietly while the men ate and drank. Soon they began to feel sleepy from the food and beer. They all crowded into the tent and their beckoning sleeping bags.

The cotton rope tied around my chest and the tree was still damp from the morning rain, especially with the humidity in the air. I knew if I put enough tension on it the cotton rope would stretch. The big question was just how much would it stretch? I thought there was a good possibility that I could saw away the pine tree bark under the rope if I could get the rope to move any. I started moving in a slight sawing motion from side to side. The bark cut into my back painfully, but I continued the motion hoping to grind down the bark both beneath the rope and behind my back. And with every movement, the rope stretched ever so slightly. It took what seemed like hours before the rope tying me to the tree was loose enough that I could begin wiggling my way out of it. I inched my torso down the tree trunk while pushing up on the rope with my upper arms. I could feel dampness on the back of my shirt from blood where the tree bark was penetrating through the skin on my back. This was a long, slow process but in the end, successful. After getting loose from the tree, I untied the ropes around my ankles. The rush of blood circulating in my feet was like a thousand pricks of an ice-pick. It was nearly impossible not to scream out, but I kept quiet. I inched along the ground toward the fire pit. There were a few embers still glowing, and I hoped to burn through the rope binding my wrists. I tried to endure the painful blisters forming on my wrist from the heat, but I gave up and decided to look for another way to free myself. It was then that I noticed the machete on the ground close to the tent. Moving as silently as possible, I crawled over to it and was able to cut through the rope and free my hands.

I slid the machete under my belt and began crawling away from the tent. All that loud snoring was music to my ears because my biggest fear at that moment was waking up my captors. I knew there was no way I could outrun them right then. I made it back to my pine tree and used it to brace myself as I got to my feet. After a couple of minutes I had enough feeling in my feet to begin slowly creeping away from camp. Using the same skills that were second nature to me when hunting, I stealthily covered about fifty yards. Then I picked up speed and began running in the direction of where I thought the car was hidden. I knew it was close to a road that I could follow. The moonlight made a huge difference as I covered unfamiliar ground.

I'd not gone far when I came to a small open field. I noticed a tree stand that looked somewhat familiar but didn't stop to check more closely. I decided to follow the tree line to my left. After following it for a while, I came upon a dirt road and then I came to an incline up to some railroad tracks. So I went back down the incline toward the dirt road where it ended at the woods. Then I started feeling around in the brush and suddenly felt metal. I started removing the brush and branches and there it was, the car. Hallelujah! This meant I could follow the dirt road, cross the railroad tracks and just ahead I'd reach the highway and safety!

I was caught up short by a sobering thought. What if Doug or the others woke up and found me gone. They could easily chase me down in the car. With no time to waste, I slashed the tires with the machete and ripped out the spark plug wires from under the hood of the car. They wouldn't be using the car to catch me!

I then headed down the dirt road. It turned and crossed over the railroad tracks. After crossing the tracks I noticed telephone poles with the old fashioned glass insulators on them. These looked familiar to me. I'd seen them where I had hunted in the past. I looked up at the night sky searching for the big dipper. Quickly I spotted it and, like my father had taught me, found the North Star. Now I knew my directions and if I was correct in guessing my location, then Greenwood would lie to the south. I followed the dirt road until I ran into the highway. So I started heading south and if I was correct there was an abandoned shack on the left side of the road. I broke into a steady trot that turned into a dead run when I spotted the shack. What a wonderful sight! I knew exactly where I was! And then I knew the gang's camp was in an area I had hunted before.

Dread lifted from me and was replaced with exhilaration! I was free, I knew where I was and I was headed in the right direction. I was safe! Suddenly the tension, fear, and fatigue hit me hard, all at once, and I burst into tears...rough, wracking sobs. And as quickly as they came, they stopped. Relief flooded through me as I realized I would soon be home. I really needed water and remembered a little country church about a mile further down the road. I continued walking south on the highway thinking of the outside faucet by the side of the church where I could get a drink.

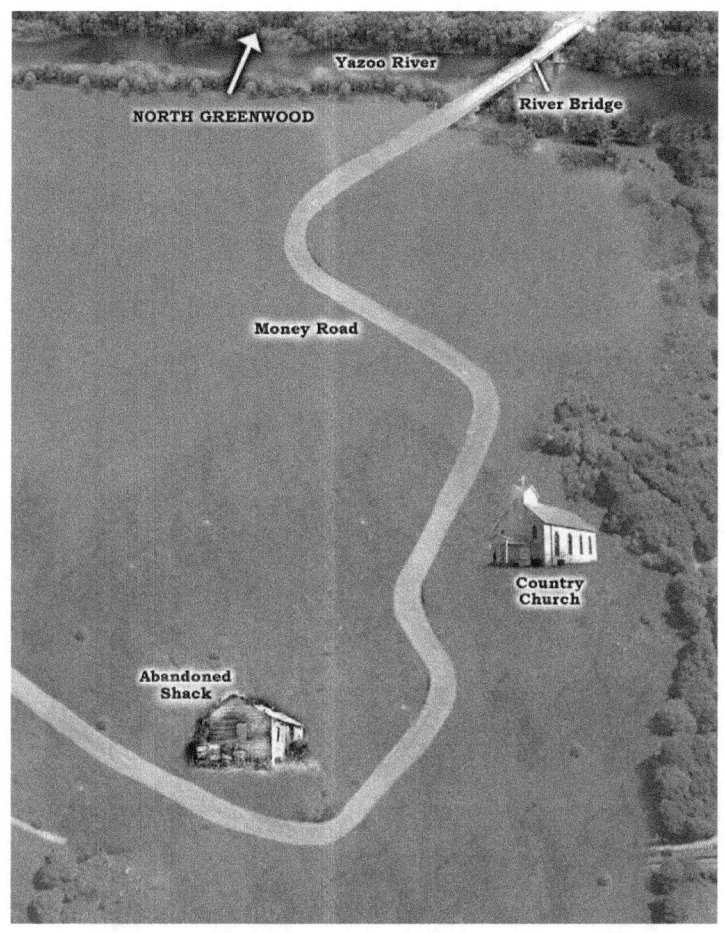

My tongue ached as the thought of drinking water filled my entire mind. When I came upon the church, I started running toward the water faucet. Then I turned it on full blast and gulped down what felt like gallons of water. Oh, how that tasted so good. I then let the water pour out over my head and face. What a relief I felt. It gave me a tremendous rush of energy and exhilaration. "Boy, I didn't know how good water could taste," I thought. Then I got back on the highway heading south toward Greenwood. My spirit was soaring as I felt the adrenalin rushing through my veins. Then I began thinking about my recent ordeal and about how quickly one's life can change. And this is where my story turns dark.

Instead of living the values learned from my parents and dwelling on the blessings of my escape, I let my thoughts turn to the evil done to me by my kidnappers. It seemed the faster I walked the more irate I became. By the time I had walked another two miles, my gut was on fire with indignation and wrath. The huge amount of cool sweet water I had just been blessed with did nothing to quench the bitterness I felt. Could I chance the kidnappers escaping? What if they were never punished for their crime? What if they hurt someone else? I couldn't just hope the police would find them; I had to do something... something to ensure that they were stopped and punished. I was at an emotional and spiritual crossroad. At that moment I remembered some words from the Bible, "Revenge is mine, saith the Lord". I realized vengeance would mean killing those four men but stopping them wouldn't. Slowly I turned around and looked back the way I had come. I began backtracking saying to myself, "...not for revenge, but for the reckoning!"

Chapter 14

I saw headlights coming toward me and slipped off the road into the woods. The car passed and I continued my trek. My mind was whirling with thoughts of my kidnappers and what I would do to them. I needed to hurt them but not kill them. I needed to disable them just like I disabled their car. I needed to make sure the authorities could find and arrest them for their crime.

It would be daylight in a couple of hours and I needed to be at the campsite before then if I was going to take anyone by surprise. I knew that even with the machete I could not take them all at the same time. Doug had his pistol and Stan his rifle, putting me at a great disadvantage. Surprise would be my best weapon. If I could get to camp before they were awake, maybe I could disarm one of them before they all realized I had escaped. Then I could hole up and wait for my next opportunity. I remembered the hollowed out cypress tree on the edge of the swamp which would be south of their camp and I was pretty sure I could find it again. That swamp was not a place my four captors were likely to go. I should be safe there and also have some protection should the weather turn bad.

I reached camp with a good half hour left before dawn. There was a heavy mist in the air which would help conceal my movements. I followed the field and turned into the woods at the tree stand and approached the gang's camp from the north working my way to the camp's look-out spot. I hid behind some heavy brush and waited. Mike was the first to awaken and step out of the tent. He came toward my hiding place never glancing over at the pine tree to which I was supposedly tied. He stepped off the path in the woods to relieve himself. He was only about three feet from me with his back facing me. I had the machete in my hand and quietly turned it blunt side up. I took a step closer to him and swung as hard as I could hitting him across his head with the broadside of the machete. Mike went limp and slumped to the ground. He was out cold. I moved quickly to remove his camouflage shirt and then checked his pants pockets. Sure enough, he was carrying his switchblade knife. I clicked it open. The wicked six inch blade was razor sharp.

Knowing I must incapacitate him completely, I used his knife to slash the Achilles tendon above his right heel. Even though unconscious, he groaned when I slashed his tendon. It would be impossible for him to walk with that injury. I tied his shirt around my waist and began moving fast toward the swamp and my hollow cypress tree which was just south of the campsite about seventy-five yards. The disabled car was a hundred yards west of the camp. The locations formed a triangle with the camp being at the eastern point. I was nestling into the cypress when I heard Mike's first screams of pain and fury. They were quickly followed by his cries for help. "One down and three to go," I thought as I settled in.

What would be their next move, I wondered. They would have to find Mike and carry him back to camp. Of course they would realize I was gone. Would they search for me on foot or try to use the car? And what about Mike? Because he couldn't walk, would they help him or just leave him at the campsite like a piece of discarded trash? All these questions were rattling around in my mind when I heard Doug's furious shout, "Where's that kid? How'd that little brat get loose?"

I hunkered further down in my hiding place pulling as many branches and leaves in with me as I could. About that time I heard the car engine as one of the men tried to start it. The engine turned over and over, but without the spark plug wires it was useless. Whoever was in the car kept trying to crank the car until the battery finally died. That part of my plan worked just as I thought, but what would be their next move?

Apparently, Harry, Stan and Doug were walking out of camp because I heard Mike shout, "Hey, somebody come help me. I can't walk on my own. You can't just leave me here!" Stan responded, "Quit your belly-aching. We gotta find the kid, and we can't do it carrying you." It was Doug who gave the orders, "All right, let's spread out and see if we can see any signs of which way he went. And if you find him, do whatever you have to. Just be sure he can't squeal on us!" Hearing that made chills run down my spine. If they found me I was dead for sure. I smeared swampy mud on my face and neck, pulled Mike's camouflage shirt over me as I blended in with my surroundings. Then I waited breathing as quietly as possible and not moving one bit.

As I think back on it now, I'm still to this day mystified that I remembered all those woodsman skills yet forgot the most important thing of all...I never prayed for God's help and protection once I was free. In such a short time, anger and vengefulness had stripped me of my strongest defense against the evil being perpetrated upon me.

Chapter 15

I dozed off inside my cypress tree. I jerked awake and sat up and realized it was early afternoon. I heard nothing other than birds, squirrels and the other small creatures living in the swamp and woods. I decided to leave my hiding place to scout around a little. I wanted some idea of where the men were. I was putting on the camouflage shirt when I heard voices from the direction of the camp. Using my hunter skills, I moved slowly and quietly in their direction. I was scanning the area all around me in case there was a look-out at the edge of camp. I got close enough to see Doug, Harry and Stan sitting outside the tent. I figured Mike must be inside.

"We've looked everywhere and can't find him," Harry complained. "Maybe he went into the swamp and an alligator got him," suggested Stan. "Or maybe he's wandering around lost in the woods. Do you think he could have made it back to the road?" Harry said, "I don't know what he did or where he is. I do know we need to get out of here before the law starts looking for us!"

Doug took command of the conversation. "If the boy had gone for help, the cops would already be here by now. He's out here somewhere, and we have to find him. You should know he's here you fool. How else would Mike have been knocked out and his ankle tendon cut? Use your stupid head for once. He can identify us. We have to find him and make sure he never talks again! After that's done then we can walk out of here to the main highway and try to catch a ride." Harry readily agreed with Doug, "Yea, if somebody gives us a ride, we can take their money and car and make a clean getaway."

Harry stepped closer to Doug and asked in a hushed voice, "What about Mike? What are we going to do about him? If we have to walk out of here, we'll have to carry him. And it sure would make it hard to hitchhike with him hurt." Doug nodded in agreement and said, "Yeah, I've been thinking about that. He'll slow us down, and we can't take him to a hospital. Even if we just leave him here, he's too dangerous. You know he'd sing like a canary if the law found him." Harry whispered, "What are you saying? Do you mean kill him, Doug? He's part of us!" Doug sneered at Harry, "You going soft, Harry? What do you think I mean, you sniveling wimp! He's no good to us now. He has to go! We'll hold off as long as we can...at least until we find the boy. Anyway, its Mike's fault that the boy escaped."

Mike was watching Doug and Harry. "Hey, what are you two whispering about? You need to get me to a hospital. Why aren't you looking for that brat? It was probably him who knocked me out and cut my leg! I want him found. I want to show him what torture really is!" Doug snarled to Mike, "Just shut up! We have to get the kid first before we can tend to you. Now keep quiet and let me think."

Doug went to a bag and rummaged through it pulling out a bottle of whiskey. He took a long drink and passed it to Harry. Mike moaned in pain as he tried to find a more comfortable position for his injured leg. "I'm sick of listening to Mike," Harry said. "He's getting on my nerves." Doug grabbed the bottle from Harry and took it to the tent. "Here Mike, have a few slugs of this. It should dull the pain," he said. Mike gulped down three big slugs of whiskey before Doug grabbed the bottle back.

Doug went back to his seat continuing to sip from the bottle passing it occasionally to Stan and Harry. "I've had it for now. I'm tired and the blasted bugs are eating me up. Hey, give me another hit off that bottle, man. Glad you had that." Doug passed Stan the bottle and the three men settled into silence. It wasn't long before Doug and Harry were in their sleeping bags snoring away. Stan decided to take the rifle and go to the lookout spot to keep an eye out for trouble.

After I saw where Stan had gone, I eased back away from camp. I stopped about thirty-five yards behind Stan. I'd picked up two sticks, one lightweight enough to throw and the other thick and strong. I then lay down beside the pathway through the woods and covered myself with brush and branches. I then threw the smaller stick behind me making enough noise to get Stan's attention. He jumped to his feet, picked up the rifle and started running along the path in my direction. Just as he got even with me, I thrust the strong stick between his legs tripping him. Just like the stick that had flipped up in the spokes of my bicycle and thrown me years before, this one did the same to Stan. He fell forward with the rifle wedged between his body and the ground. The instant he hit the ground, I jumped up and straddled his back. I jabbed the switchblade into his leg up to the hilt and twisted it as hard as I could hoping to tear his femoral artery. Stan let out a blood curdling scream. I quickly reached around his neck grabbing his Adam's apple. I squeezed it hard. Stan let go of the rifle as he scrambled to get my hands off his throat. I jumped up rolling Stan off the rifle. As he was holding his throat and gasping for air, I grabbed the rifle and bashed him in the head with the butt. I hurried away from camp as fast as I could without making any noise. My last glance at Stan told me he was no danger to me just now. Blood was pooling under his wounded leg, and he still labored to breathe.

Chapter 16

Doug and Harry crashed through the woods searching for Stan. I knew they needed to find him soon and attend to his leg wound before he bled out. That would give me time to get a safe distance away from them. Then I heard Harry yell, "Doug, over here. I found him." I began circling around back to the safety of my cypress tree. All the while I heard bits and pieces of conversation and more than a few pain-filled curses from Stan as he was taken back to the campsite.

After a little time passed, I decided to have a look at the situation in camp. I inched my way closer and could see Doug and Harry sitting by a big roaring campfire. In the glow from the campfire, I saw that Stan was in the tent with Mike. There was a tourniquet around his leg, but the pale, ashen pallor of his face told me he'd lost a lot of blood. He must be getting cold from the loss of blood.

Doug and Harry were sullen and angry as they discussed their situation. "We need to find that punk, Doug," Harry whined. "I know that, stupid!

But we can't do it now. It's getting dark and we'll get lost. Come morning we'll start a methodical sweep of this whole area. We're bound to find him," Doug retorted. "But Doug, he's got the rifle now!" Harry exclaimed. Doug's reply was cold and flat, "Yes he does. But I have the pistol and plenty of ammunition."

I eased my way back to the cypress tree, crawled in and slept. When I awoke, the moon had risen but was not far above the horizon. I took the rifle and began making my way back to the camp area. When I got close enough to see into camp, all four men were in the tent. Probably Doug and Harry got tired of fighting the mosquitoes. Then the next step of my plan for reckoning hit me.

Keeping the rifle with me in case I got caught, I crawled on my belly to the campfire. It was burning low and the men were asleep. I slid a somewhat long branch out of the fire. It was burning slowly on one end leaving the other end cool enough to hold in my hand. I moved quickly then with the rifle in one hand and the branch in the other and headed for the back of the tent. I laid the burning branch against the tent fabric. I slinked back into the woods looking for a good tree to climb.

It didn't take long to find a tree I wanted, and I was perched high in it when I heard the first shouts from the gang. Through the branches in the woods, I saw the back half of the tent ablaze. Harry and Doug were pulling Mike and Stan from the tent. They were barely out when I saw the tent rise up like a fireball and vanish in a poof of ash and smoke.

Doug and Harry were visibly stunned and confused. They stumbled toward the campfire and their chairs. I raised the rifle and watched the scene through the scope. Suddenly I had Harry's thigh in the crosshairs. With no hesitation I squeezed the trigger and Harry folded to the ground with blood spurting from the wound in his thigh. Not taking time to help Harry, Doug scurried out of the firelight. He was yelling curses and challenges at me, "You lousy sneak! Come out here and face me like a man!"

I settled down in the tree to wait. The moon had just passed the crest of the night sky when I made my next move. I climbed down the tree and crept along the ground and circled around to the north side of the camp. Coming in close enough to the camp to see, there were three deflated, angry men with painful leg injuries and one dejected yet furious gang leader who now had no one to order or lead.

Doug had gone closer to the campfire and was again gulping down beer. As I watched, his head began to nod as sleep overtook him. I smiled to myself as I eased back away from the scene. When I got a safe distance back, I found another good climbing tree and shinnied up it. I looked through the rifle scope and watched the fitfully sleeping, miserable man. He was on the other side of the campfire from me. "No more sleep for you tonight," I whispered as I sighted through the scope. I squeezed off a shot that hit dead center of a blazing log. The log exploded showering Doug with hot coals. Doug jumped up from his chair brushing hot embers off his shirt and pants. Then with a primordial scream he started running in my direction. He fired three shots from the pistol...POW, POW, POW...calling out, "Come on out you little coward!" He ran a short way into the woods, then retreated back to camp. I smiled again as I thought, "That will keep them up for a while. I then climbed down and went to the tree-stand I had seen and used in the past to take a nap. Like my father had taught me, I made sure I was squeezed in between some limbs so I wouldn't fall. After dozing for a period of time, I checked the gang out again to see how they were doing. They were starting to nod off. The moon was full in the sky so I got a running start in the woods and darted through their campsite shrieking at the top of my lungs. I was out of the camp as fast as I entered it, back into the dark woods. The gang was so startled, they hollered out as they struggled to get to safety. I must have looked a fright to them, a wild banshee running through the campsite. A smile crept over my face again.

I slinked back to the cypress tree where I took stock of the situation...no tent for protection, three incapacitating leg wounds, no hostage, awake in fright for the rest of the night...a good nights' work.

Before getting inside the cypress, I smeared myself with more mud to ward off the mosquitoes. Those Arkansas guys would not know that trick. Tonight they would be nothing more than a living buffet for Mississippi mosquitoes and they deserved every painful bite they got. In the safety of my cypress nest I dozed off to sleep thinking of the possibilities to come in the morning.

Chapter 17

Dawn was breaking when I woke up. It had rained during the night. The air was heavy with mist giving the woods an eerie light. I had to come up with another plan for dealing with Doug. I knew he had fired three shots from his pistol leaving three remaining bullets. I didn't know if he had additional ammunition for reloading although I could not imagine that he would have undertaken this kidnapping without it. I had fired two rounds from the rifle leaving three unused. I would have to use those wisely saving them as a last line of defense. I decided to leave the machete and rifle in the cypress tree and take only the switchblade so I could move more quickly and stealthily as I set out to assess the conditions in the camp.

I crept silently to a vantage point from which I could see all four men. They were bunched together on the ground trying to warm themselves. They were soggy wet from the night's rain. Doug looked bleary eyed and exhausted. He'd most likely not slept at all. The other three obviously in pain and suffering the effects of their injuries and blood loss. They were all shivering from the damp and, I suspected, from fevers. All three of them were likely developing infections from their wounds.

As I watched them, I saw that Doug was settling down to sleep. I imagined he felt daylight offered him a window of safety. I was going to make sure that was not the case. When I was sure Doug was sleeping, I slipped further back from camp and circled around to the pine tree where I had been tied. As I had hoped, the rope used to tie me to the tree was still lying there on the ground. I picked up the rope and returned to the cypress tree to get ready for my next assault.

I tied two pieces of the rope together forming a twelve foot length. In my plan I would need to get Doug to follow me and go into the swamp. I headed closer to the swampy bog and began scouting around for a deer path. It didn't take long to find one. I was pretty sure Doug would not go deep into the swamp out of fear. It would be totally unknown territory to someone from the Ozark Mountains. I only needed for him to go a short way in. When he hit the thick mud, he'd want to get out of it. He'd surely spot the deer path and follow it because it was easier to travel.

Not far from the edge of the swamp along the deer path I found two trees parallel to each other with the deer path running between them. Here was my perfect spot for Doug's undoing! I tied the rope to the base of the two trees about four inches above the ground. Then I set about covering the rope with dirt and leaves. If my plan worked, Doug would be exhausted after slogging through the gumbo in the swamp and would be dragging his feet along the deer path. The rope would trip him up causing him to fall flat on his face. Then it occurred to me that a fall was not enough punishment nor would it incapacitate him. That's when I got creative and came up with my next injury producing idea.

Within a couple of minutes I had collected half a dozen sturdy sticks about six inches long. Using the switchblade, I whittled the ends into sharp points making Punji sticks of them. I then estimated how far from the rope Doug's thighs would hit the ground when he tripped and fell. I drove the Punji sticks into the ground where his thighs would hit when he tripped and fell. If the plan worked, when Doug fell onto the Punji sticks, they would tear through his pants and jam into his thighs. I covered them with a few leaves so they were not so noticeable. With that trap laid and ready, I headed to the north side of their camp.

The rain had doused the campfire. The gang was still huddled together on the ground and Doug appeared to be sleeping. I did not see his pistol and thought he most likely had put it under his shirt in the waistband of his pants to keep it dry. As I looked at my captors and thought of what they had done to me, I felt a deep, primal need to punish them. I wanted to make them feel small and defenseless. It was then that I remembered reading about counting coup. I'd read about American Indians using this tactic to show their fearlessness and superiority against a bear during a hunt. They would run quickly by the bear, smack it on the head with a branch, then run away before the bear could react. Yes, by George, I was going to count coup on old Doug. He needed a good dose of humiliation.

I moved silently in by circling camp and coming from north of the four men. I'd picked up a good sized branch and clutched it tight in my hands. Suddenly I broke into a dead run screaming at the top of my lungs. As I ran past the group, I hit Doug as hard as I could on the side of his head as he was trying to get up. I then brought the branch down hard on the legs of the three others. Before Doug could get back up I ran whooping toward the woods and fell silent.

I stopped at the edge of the clearing and saw Doug struggling to his feet. He seemed dazed from the blow to his head. Spotting me standing at the edge, Mike yelled, "Over there, Doug! Shoot him!" Doug was fumbling for the pistol as he started in my direction. I turned toward the swamp running fast. I zigzagged through the trees and heard a shot ring out. "Two bullets left if I'm lucky and he hasn't reloaded," I thought to myself. Doug was crashing through the trees in hot pursuit of me, but the misty haze made me more difficult to see. I paused a moment to catch sight of Doug. After I was sure he could get a glimpse of me, I ran on leading him to the swamp. The hazy air reminded me of the morning I saw the "ghost deer" a couple of years before. I must have looked that same way to Doug.

When I reached the swamp I turned east along its edge to the deer path. I threw a big stick as far into the swamp as I could to divert Doug's attention. He fell for the trick and I could hear him splashing in the shallow water as he entered the swamp. It was hard not to taunt Doug as he slogged through the mud and water. I could hear him cursing as he was battling the sludge through the swamp. I would have given anything to see his face when he first realized he was in the home territory of alligators and water moccasins. No matter how frightened he might be, there was no way he could run through that muck. He'd be lucky not to lose his shoes.

I watched from the woods as Doug struggled. As was bound to happen, he lost his balance and fell into that stinky sludge. When he was back on his feet he was covered in sticky green slime. I wondered if any swamp trash had gotten into his gun barrel. If it had plugged up the pistol barrel and he shot again, it could conceivably blow up in his face. I remember thinking, "It would serve him right!" How far down the path of revenge I had traveled.

Doug reversed direction to get out of the swamp. When he got to solid ground, I saw him looking around trying to get his bearings. He spied the deer path, and just as I anticipated, he started walking on it. I could tell he was exhausted from lack of sleep and the swamp excursion, so he was predictably shuffling along the deer trail. He soon reached the booby trap, and it worked like a charm. He tripped and fell forward landing with a thud on the Punji sticks. His shrill screams pierced the air as the sticks drove into the flesh of his thighs.

In an instinctive reaction, Doug dropped the pistol and grabbed for his wounded legs. As he pushed himself up and onto his knees, I could see three sticks protruding from his legs...one from the right leg and two from the left leg. He stared at the sticks in disbelief for a moment, then one by one pulled them out. As each Punji stick was extracted from Doug's quivering thighs, it was like pulling a cork from a full keg. Blood spurted out forming ever widening rivulets down to his knees and into the dirt path. Not even attempting to stand, Doug began crawling on all fours down the path he hoped would lead him back to camp.

Chapter 18

I heard Doug hollering out to his gang because he was having trouble finding camp. The others hollered back so that he could follow the sound of their voices. By the time Doug had crawled to camp, the sun had burned off the morning mist and turned the atmosphere into a sauna. This was going to be one of those scorching Mississippi Indian summer days. There would be no relief for any of us, but my advantage was that I was no stranger to such days, unlike my mountaineer captors.

Upon hearing Doug relate the story of what happened to him, I returned to the trap to retrieve the pistol Doug had dropped on the path and started back to their campsite. Keeping out of their line of vision, I slid their cooler to the edge of the woods. Inside were a few beers, a small block of cheese and a jug of water. I downed half the water and some of the cheese. Then I moved the cooler further into the woods and hid it. The gang would have no food or beverage today. A little more misery would serve them right. They needed to feel some of what they put me through.

Stan was pleading with Mike, "Can't you use a limb to make a crutch and make it to the road? You could flag down a car and get us help." Mike spat back, "And just what would I tell anybody? We shot and mutilated ourselves and now we can't walk! Oh and by the way, we burned down our tent and disabled our car just for fun? You're such an idiot!" Harry joined in, "But if we don't get help soon, we're all going to die out here!" Mike responded, "Its Doug's fault. He should have let me kill that kid when I wanted to."

I listened to the squabbling for a while and then decided it was time for a little more fun. I thought some guerrilla warfare would make for a nice game. Doug had the slightest injury of the four and, therefore, was the most dangerous. With three puncture wounds in his thighs, he could possibly still manage to walk. I made up my mind to use the pistol on him. I had already checked to be sure the barrel was clear before I eased up to the campsite. I then took aim, squeezed the trigger and splintered Doug's right knee. As he was screaming in surprise and pain, I stuffed the pistol into the cooler for safe keeping so I could hand it over to the police later.

I had done it. I had bested four grown men. I had made them suffer. I had put their lives in danger. Now it was time for the game to end. But I smiled as I remembered all the fun I'd had outsmarting that gang.

I followed the dirt road, went over the railroad tracks and went to the highway once again and started walking toward Greenwood. After a few minutes I flagged down a ride. I told the driver I needed to go to the Greenwood Police Station. In just a few short minutes, I was there.

Conclusion

The first thing I did at the Police Station was call home to let my family know I was safe. I told them where I was and assured them I was not hurt. I told them a cruiser would take me home after I showed the officers where the kidnappers were located. I told my story to the police detective on duty and we set out to locate the campsite. I had no trouble taking them right to the site.

Doug, Harry, Stan and Mike were taken to the hospital by ambulance. I turned over the switchblade in my pocket and the pistol in the cooler. An officer and I retrieved the rifle and machete from my cypress tree. While the camp area was being investigated, the detective drove me home. I was a little puzzled by his comment to me, "I'm amazed that you were able to get free of those men and do all the things to them that you did. But, knowing you and your family, I'm really surprised that you did those things at all." It wasn't until later that I understood what he was actually saying to me.

As the police car pulled up to the house, my parents and Alma were all running to greet me. There were hugs and joyful tears on all their faces. Even Mr. LaRoche was sniffling. We all went inside and straight to the kitchen. While Alma was making me eggs and bacon, I began to recount the story of my kidnapping and escape. I was very excited and was laughing as I told about how I had dreamed up ways to injure each man. I felt so proud of myself.

As I told my story, the room became very quiet. I noticed Mr. LaRoche look a little uncomfortable, and midway into my account of my exploits, he excused himself saying he needed to get back to his office. The look on his face seemed like he was embarrassed. It confused me.

I looked at my parents and saw such a mixture of expressions on their faces. There was, of course, relief and thankfulness. But there was something more. As I looked into my father's eyes, I saw sadness. In my mother's eyes I saw pain. What was this all about? I didn't understand. I looked over at Alma hoping for some explanation. She dipped her head and turned back to her cooking.

My father was the one to break the silence in the room,"I think we need to have a time of prayer now." We all bowed our heads as father prayed, "Heavenly Father, we come to you in thanksgiving for the safe return of Ron to us. We give you the praise and glory for it. Also, Lord, we pray for the four men who took him as they lay wounded in the hospital. Watch over them, and if it is within your will, may they be healed. We pray in the name of your Son, Jesus Christ. Amen."

As I heard my father utter that simple prayer, I was hit with the gravity of what I had done. I had let hate and vengefulness displace love and dependence on God in my heart. I had not turned the other cheek. When I first escaped, I could and should have gone straight into Greenwood to the police. I should not have gone down that path of Reckoning. Not only had I mistreated the kidnappers, I had prolonged my parents' misery for many unnecessary hours. How wrong I had been!

Tears welled up in my eyes as I felt the shame of what I had done. Looking at my parents I said, "I'm going to get a shower and then go to the hospital. I have some unfinished business there. I must right some wrongs...or at least try to."

When I arrived at the hospital, I learned that each of the men were in a separate room. All had police officers guarding their rooms. When I went into each man, I apologized for the injuries I had inflicted and for not showing Christian compassion for them like I should. Doug, Stan and Harry were not receptive to me, each ordering me from their room. Their language was abusive and vulgar, but I did not respond in kind.

I expected Mike to be the toughest on me of them all. When I went into his room and told him I was sorry for my actions and asked his forgiveness, he asked me why. I explained, "Jesus, the Son of God, died for my sins. I have been forgiven. And as a born again Christian, I should have forgiven you." Mike asked me what I meant about Jesus. I told him the story of Jesus and that God had sent Jesus to earth as a sacrifice for the sins of all who believe in him. I went on to explain that when I accepted Jesus, the Holy Spirit came to dwell in my heart. I told Mike that Jesus is the example by which we should live our lives and that I was wrong to take revenge on him. Mike began to cry saying he wanted to know this Jesus. I led Mike in the prayer of repentance. Lying in his hospital bed, Mike accepted the Lord Jesus as his personal savior. Mike listened as I prayed for God's forgiveness for my own sins. I felt the guilt of my actions lift from my shoulders as that forgiveness was granted.

At supper that night, I told my folks and Alma about visiting the hospital and about what happened with each of the men. I then thanked them for their love, prayers and years of guidance. I told them how sorry I was that I had fallen prey to hateful, evil feelings and that I knew I had disappointed them. My father spoke, "Ron, I'm sure I can speak for your mother and Alma too when I say to you that I have never been any prouder of you in your life than I am at this moment. You are a true child of God."

So that is my tale. It's been ten years ago now. I stay in touch with Mike. He was released from prison early due to his good behavior while there. He was active in starting up a Christian fellowship in the prison. In fact, I'll see him later this week when we speak to a group at the Mississippi Youth Offenders Facility. We share our story with as many youth groups as possible. Keeping young people off the wrong path is our goal.

Eustus Bogan was the first person to invite Mike and me to speak to a youth group... actually that invitation may have been more of Alma's quiet work. I'll never know unless she decides to sing a song about it.

About the Authors

Ronald Williamson was born in Greenville, MS, and moved to Greenwood, MS, during grade school. He attended North Greenwood Baptist Church where he accepted Jesus as his savior and was baptized. Ron moved around quite a bit and later joined the U.S. Army in 1984 and was stationed in Büdingen, West Germany, where he married and had a son, Chad Lee Williamson. After leaving the Army, Ron and his family moved around and while living in Evanston, Wyoming, attended a Baptist Church where his son Chad accepted Jesus as his savior and was baptized. Ron continued moving to a variety of states and is currently residing in Millbrook, Alabama, with his wife Lea. They are current members of a Baptist Church and are both anxiously waiting for that blessed hope, Jesus Christ, to return soon and rapture the Church.

Carolyn Clark assisted the Author in creating this work of fiction. A lifelong resident of the south, Carolyn has lived in Georgia, Tennessee, Louisiana, and now resides in Millbrook, Alabama.

She is a member of St. Michael's and All Angels Episcopal Church and is the mother of Ron's wife, Lea.